DATE			

B 23497284 79
P 215 258.67

30

BAKER & TAYLOR

María Dolores Costa
Editor

Latina Lesbian
Writers and Artists

Latina Lesbian Writers and Artists has been co-published simultaneously as *Journal of Lesbian Studies*, Volume 7, Number 3 2003.

Pre-publication
REVIEWS,
COMMENTARIES,
EVALUATIONS . . .

" A fascinating journey through the Latina lesbian experience. It brings us stories of exile, assimilation, and conflict of cultures. The book takes us to the Midwest, New York, Chicana Borderlands, Mexico, Argentina, and Spain. It succeeds at showing the diversity within the Latina lesbian experience through deeply feminist testimonials of life and struggle."

Susana Cook
Performance Artist and Playwright

Latina Lesbian Writers and Artists

Latina Lesbian Writers and Artists has been co-published simultaneously as *Journal of Lesbian Studies*, Volume 7, Number 3 2003.

The *Journal of Lesbian Studies* Monographic "Separates"

Below is a list of "separates," which in serials librarianship means a special issue simultaneously published as a special journal issue or double-issue *and* as a "separate" hardbound monograph. (This is a format which we also call a "DocuSerial.")

"Separates" are published because specialized libraries or professionals may wish to purchase a specific thematic issue by itself in a format which can be separately cataloged and shelved, as opposed to purchasing the journal on an on-going basis. Faculty members may also more easily consider a "separate" for classroom adoption.

"Separates" are carefully classified separately with the major book jobbers so that the journal tie-in can be noted on new book order slips to avoid duplicate purchasing.

You may wish to visit Haworth's website at . . .

http://www.HaworthPress.com

. . . to search our online catalog for complete tables of contents of these separates and related publications.

You may also call 1-800-HAWORTH (outside US/Canada: 607-722-5857), or Fax 1-800-895-0582 (outside US/Canada: 607-771-0012), or e-mail at:

docdelivery@haworthpress.com

Latina Lesbian Writers and Artists, edited by María Dolores Costa, PhD (Vol. 7, No. 3, 2003). *"A fascinating journey through the Latina lesbian experience. It brings us stories of exile, assimilation, and conflict of cultures. The book takes us to the Midwest, New York, Chicana Borderlands, Mexico, Argentina, and Spain. It succeeds at showing the diversity within the Latina lesbian experience through deeply feminist testimonials of life and struggle."* (Susana Cook, performance artist and playwright)

Lesbian Rites: Symbolic Acts and the Power of Community, edited by Ramona Faith Oswald, PhD (Vol. 7, No. 2, 2003). *"Informative, enlightening, and well written . . . illuminates the range of lesbian ritual behavior in a creative and thorough manner. Ramona Faith Oswald and the contributors to this book have done scholars and students of ritual studies an important service by demonstrating the power, pervasiveness, and performative nature of lesbian ritual practices."* (Cele Otnes, PhD, Associate Professor, Department of Business Administration, University of Illinois)

Mental Health Issues for Sexual Minority Women: Redefining Women's Mental Health, edited by Tonda L. Hughes, RN, PhD, FAAN, Carrol Smith, RN, MS, and Alice Dan, PhD (Vol. 7, No. 1, 2003). *A rare look at mental health issues for lesbians and other sexual minority women.*

Addressing Homophobia and Heterosexism on College Campuses, edited by Elizabeth P. Cramer, PhD (Vol. 6, No. 3/4, 2002). *A practical guide to creating LGBT-supportive environments on college campuses.*

Femme/Butch: New Considerations of the Way We Want to Go, edited by Michelle Gibson and Deborah T. Meem (Vol. 6, No. 2, 2002). *"Disrupts the fictions of heterosexual norms. . . . A much-needed examiniation of the ways that butch/femme identitites subvert both heteronormativity and 'expected' lesbian behavior."* (Patti Capel Swartz, PhD, Assistant Professor of English, Kent State University)

Lesbian Love and Relationships, edited by Suzanna M. Rose, PhD (Vol. 6, No. 1, 2002). *"Suzanna Rose's collection of 13 essays is well suited to prompting serious contemplation and discussion about lesbian lives and how they are–or are not–different from others. . . . Interesting and useful for debunking some myths, confirming others, and reaching out into new territories that were previously unexplored."* (Lisa Keen, BA, MFA, Senior Political Correspondent, Washington Blade)

Everyday Mutinies: Funding Lesbian Activism, edited by Nanette K. Gartrell, MD, and Esther D. Rothblum, PhD (Vol. 5, No. 3, 2001). *"Any lesbian who fears she'll never find the money, time, or support for her work can take heart from the resourcefulness and dogged determination of the contributors to this book. Not only do these inspiring stories provide practical tips on making dreams come true, they offer an informal history of lesbian political activism since World War II." (Jane Futcher, MA, Reporter,* Marin Independent Journal, *and author of* Crush, Dream Lover, *and* Promise Not to Tell)

Lesbian Studies in Aotearoa/New Zealand, edited by Alison J. Laurie (Vol. 5, No. 1/2, 2001). *These fascinating studies analyze topics ranging from the gender transgressions of women passing as men in order to work and marry as they wished to the effects of coming out on modern women's health.*

Lesbian Self-Writing: The Embodiment of Experience, edited by Lynda Hall (Vol. 4, No. 4, 2000). *"Probes the intersection of love for words and love for women. . . . Luminous, erotic, evocative." (Beverly Burch, PhD, psychotherapist and author,* Other Women: Lesbian/Bisexual Experience and Psychoanalytic Views of Women *and* On Intimate Terms: The Psychology of Difference in Lesbian Relationships)

'Romancing the Margins'? Lesbian Writing in the 1990s, edited by Gabriele Griffin, PhD (Vol. 4, No. 2, 2000). *Explores lesbian issues through the mediums of books, movies, and poetry and offers readers critical essays that examine current lesbian writing and discuss how recent movements have tried to remove racist and anti-gay themes from literature and movies.*

From Nowhere to Everywhere: Lesbian Geographies, edited by Gill Valentine, PhD (Vol. 4, No. 1, 2000). *"A significant and worthy contribution to the ever growing literature on sexuality and space. . . . A politically significant volume representing the first major collection on lesbian geographies. . . . I will make extensive use of this book in my courses on social and cultural geography and sexuality and space." (Jon Binnie, PhD, Lecturer in Human Geography, Liverpool, John Moores University, United Kingdom)*

Lesbians, Levis and Lipstick: The Meaning of Beauty in Our Lives, edited by Jeanine C. Cogan, PhD, and Joanie M. Erickson (Vol. 3, No. 4, 1999). *Explores lesbian beauty norms and the effects these norms have on lesbian women.*

Lesbian Sex Scandals: Sexual Practices, Identities, and Politics, edited by Dawn Atkins, MA (Vol. 3, No. 3, 1999). *"Grounded in material practices, this collection explores confrontation and coincidence among identity politics, 'scandalous' sexual practices, and queer theory and feminism. . . . It expands notions of lesbian identification and lesbian community." (Maria Pramaggiore, PhD, Assistant Professor, Film Studies, North Carolina State University, Raleigh)*

The Lesbian Polyamory Reader: Open Relationships, Non-Monogamy, and Casual Sex, edited by Marcia Munson and Judith P. Stelboum, PhD (Vol. 3, No. 1/2, 1999). *"Offers reasonable, logical, and persuasive explanations for a style of life I had not seriously considered before. . . . A terrific read." (Beverly Todd, Acquisitions Librarian, Estes Park Public Library, Estes Park, Colorado)*

Living "Difference": Lesbian Perspectives on Work and Family Life, edited by Gillian A. Dunne, PhD (Vol. 2, No. 4, 1998). *"A fascinating, groundbreaking collection. . . . Students and professionals in psychiatry, psychology, sociology, and anthropology will find this work extremely useful and thought provoking." (Nanette K. Gartrell, MD, Associate Clinical Professor of Psychiatry, University of California at San Francisco Medical School)*

Acts of Passion: Sexuality, Gender, and Performance, edited by Nina Rapi, MA, and Maya Chowdhry, MA (Vol. 2, No. 2/3, 1998). *"This significant and impressive publication draws together a diversity of positions, practices, and polemics in relation to postmodern lesbian performance and puts them firmly on the contemporary cultural map." (Lois Keidan, Director of Live Arts, Institute of Contemporary Arts, London, United Kingdom)*

Gateways to Improving Lesbian Health and Health Care: Opening Doors, edited by Christy M. Ponticelli, PhD (Vol. 2, No. 1, 1997). *"An unprecedented collection that goes to the source for powerful and poignant information on the state of lesbian health care." (Jocelyn C. White, MD, Assistant Professor of Medicine, Oregon Health Sciences University; Faculty, Portland Program in General Internal Medicine, Legacy Portland Hospitals, Portland, Oregon)*

Classics in Lesbian Studies, edited by Esther Rothblum, PhD (Vol. 1, No. 1, 1996). *"Brings together a collection of powerful chapters that cross disciplines and offer a broad vision of lesbian lives across race, age, and community." (Michele J. Eliason, PhD, Associate Professor, College of Nursing, The University of Iowa)*

∞ ALL HARRINGTON PARK PRESS BOOKS
AND JOURNALS ARE PRINTED
ON CERTIFIED ACID-FREE PAPER

Latina Lesbian
Writers and Artists

María Dolores Costa, PhD
Editor

Latina Lesbian Writers and Artists has been co-published simultaneously
as *Journal of Lesbian Studies*, Volume 7, Number 3 2003.

Harrington Park Press
An Imprint of
The Haworth Press, Inc.
New York • London • Oxford

Published by

Harrington Park Press®, 10 Alice Street, Binghamton, NY 13904-1580 USA

Harrington Park Press® is an imprint of The Haworth Press, Inc., 10 Alice Street, Binghamton, NY 13904-1580 USA.

Latina Lesbian Writers and Artists has been co-published simultaneously as *Journal of Lesbian Studies*, Volume 7, Number 3 2003.

The development, preparation, and publication of this work has been undertaken with great care. However, the publisher, employees, editors, and agents of The Haworth Press and all imprints of The Haworth Press, Inc., including The Haworth Medical Press® and The Pharmaceutical Products Press®, are not responsible for any errors contained herein or for consequences that may ensue from use of materials or information contained in this work. Opinions expressed by the author(s) are not necessarily those of The Haworth Press, Inc. With regard to case studies, identities and circumstances of individuals discussed herein have been changed to protect confidentiality. Any resemblance to actual persons, living or dead, is entirely coincidental.

Cover illustration by Tonya López-Craig

Cover design by Brooke R. Stiles

Library of Congress Cataloging-in-Publication Data

Latina lesbian writers and artists / Maria Dolores Costa, editor.
      p.   cm.
   ". . . co-published simultaneously as Journal of Lesbian Studies, Volume 7, Number 3 2003."
   Includes bibliographical references and index.
   ISBN 1-56023-278-1 (hard cover : alk. paper) – ISBN 1-56023-279-X (soft cover : alk. paper)
   1. Lesbians' writings, American–History and criticism. 2. American literature–Hispanic American authors–History and criticism. 3. Spanish American literature–Women authors–History and criticism. 4. American literature–Women authors–History and criticism. 5. Lesbians' writings, Spanish American–History and criticism. 6. Spanish literature–Women authors–History and criticism. 7. 8. Lesbian artists. I. Costa, Maria Dolores. II. Journal of lesbian studies.
   PS153.L46L36 2003
   700'.89'68073–dc21
                                                                                    2003010589

Indexing, Abstracting & Website/Internet Coverage

This section provides you with a list of major indexing & abstracting services. That is to say, each service began covering this periodical during the year noted in the right column. Most Websites which are listed below have indicated that they will either post, disseminate, compile, archive, cite or alter their own Website users with research-based content from this work. (This list is as current as the copyright date of this publication.)

Abstracting, Website/Indexing Coverage . . . . Year When Coverage Began

- *Abstracts in Social Gerontology: Current Literature*
  on Aging **1997**

- *CNPIEC Reference Guide: Chinese National Directory*
  of Foreign Periodicals **1997**

- *Contemporary Women's Issues* **1998**

- *e-psyche, LLC <www.e-psyche.net>* **2001**

- *Family Index Database <www.familyscholar.com>* **2003**

- *Family & Society Studies Worldwide <www.nisc.com>* **2001**

- *Feminist Periodicals: A Current Listing of Contents* **1997**

- *Gay & Lesbian Abstracts <www.nisc.com>* **1997**

- *GenderWatch <www.slinfo.com>* **1999**

- *HOMODOK/"Relevant" Bibliographic database,*
  Documentation Centre for Gay & Lesbian Studies,
  University of Amsterdam (selective printed abstracts
  in "Homologie" and bibliographic computer databases
  covering cultural, historical, social, and political aspects
  of gay & lesbian topics) **1997**

(continued)

Special Bibliographic Notes related to special journal issues (separates) and indexing/abstracting:

- indexing/abstracting services in this list will also cover material in any "separate" that is co-published simultaneously with Haworth's special thematic journal issue or DocuSerial. Indexing/abstracting usually covers material at the article/chapter level.
- monographic co-editions are intended for either non-subscribers or libraries which intend to purchase a second copy for their circulating collections.
- monographic co-editions are reported to all jobbers/wholesalers/approval plans. The source journal is listed as the "series" to assist the prevention of duplicate purchasing in the same manner utilized for books-in-series.
- to facilitate user/access services all indexing/abstracting services are encouraged to utilize the co-indexing entry note indicated at the bottom of the first page of each article/chapter/contribution.
- this is intended to assist a library user of any reference tool (whether print, electronic, online, or CD-ROM) to locate the monographic version if the library has purchased this version but not a subscription to the source journal.
- individual articles/chapters in any Haworth publication are also available through the Haworth Document Delivery Service (HDDS).

Latina Lesbian Writers and Artists

CONTENTS

ABOUT THE EDITOR

María Dolores Costa, PhD, is Professor of Spanish at California State University, Los Angeles, where she mostly teaches heritage learners of Spanish. She received her PhD from the University of Massachusetts, Amherst, and her BA and MA from Kent State University. Her area of specialization is nineteenth and twentieth century narrative. She has taught courses on women's writing, the literature of the Spanish Civil War, nature in Spanish literature, and spirituality in Spanish literature. She has published articles and delivered papers on numerous topics, including feminism and ecofeminism, pedagogy, Chicano and Hispanic films, Spanish gay and lesbian writers, and Spanish authors Federico García Lorca, Rosalía de Castro, Ramón del Valle-Inclán, Julio Camba, Arturo Barea, and Benito Pérez-Galdós. She is currently working on a book about Spanish nature writing from Romanticism to the present. She has also published several book reviews, predominantly on lesbian themes. Beyond her academic pursuits, she is involved with the Quaker faith, and has published some pieces in Quaker publications.

Introduction

María Dolores Costa

This volume is intended to serve as an introduction to Latina lesbian literature, art, and performance. It does not provide, by any stretch of the imagination, a comprehensive look at the many works, writers, and performers that
form what we could call the Latina lesbian canon–a canon which, happily, is
flourishing and growing today. What it hopefully does do is familiarize the
reader with some of the important and innovative work being produced by
Latina lesbians and with the textual strategies lesbian authors, texts, and readers have brought to the study of Hispanic literature and art.

We begin with an overview of recent Latina lesbian authors and performers,
along with some bibliographical references for further research. The rest of the
volume is structured so that we first look at Latina lesbian production in the
United States, then move geographically outward, first to Latin America, then to
Spain.

"Tortilleras on the Prairie: Latina Lesbians Writing the Midwest" gives us a
unique look at a much-neglected component of Latina lesbian writing (and, indeed, Latina writing)–that of the Latinas living far from the East Coast and West
Coast hubs of both Latino and queer cultures. Since what we think about Latina
lesbians is garnered largely from our observations of those based in California or
the New York area, a careful glance at the literary production of those based in
places like Kansas or Nebraska will necessarily revise our perceptions.

"The Role of Carmelita Tropicana in the Performance Art of Alina Troyano"
appraises the imaginative work of Cuban-American performance artist

[Haworth co-indexing entry note]: "Introduction." Costa. María Dolores. Co-published simultaneously in *Journal of Lesbian Studies* (Harrington Park Press, an imprint of The Haworth Press, Inc.) Vol. 7, No. 3, 2003, pp. 1-2;
and: *Latina Lesbian Writers and Artists* (ed: María Dolores Costa) Harrington Park Press, an imprint of The Haworth
Press, Inc., 2003, pp. 1-2. Single or multiple copies of this article are available for a fee from The Haworth Document Delivery Service [1-800-HAWORTH, 9:00 a.m. - 5:00 p.m. (EST). E-mail address: docdelivery@
haworthpress.com].

http://www.haworthpress.com/store/product.asp?sku=J155
10.1300/J155v07n03_01

Carmelita Tropicana, arriving at the conclusion that her work cannot be easily labeled–as Latina lesbian or Latina–because it is persistently marked by otherness. The article also hints at why performance art is such a valuable means of expression for Latina lesbians.

"Moving *La Frontera* Towards a Genuine Radical Democracy in Gloria Anzaldúa's Work" shows us how *Borderlands*, Anzaldúa's pivotal work, has revolutionized academic readings–and academic readers–of the border and identity in the field of Latin American/U.S. Latino literature.

"Como Sabes, Depresión" is a passionate bilingual poem written by a poet enamored of the Spanish language, while "To Sor Juana" is a poem dedicated to the seventeenth century poet and nun who (along with Frida Kahlo, another notable Mexican woman) has become something of an icon among Latina lesbians.

In "Lesbianism and Caricature in Griselda Gambaro's *Lo impenetrable*," we see how lesbian characters and themes in the works of this Argentine novelist are used to satirize and undermine the perverse social values of patriarchal dictatorship.

We conclude with "The (In)visible Lesbian: The Contradictory Representations of Female Homoeroticism in Contemporary Spain," which introduces us to some of Spain's lesbian authors and communicates the difficulties lesbian writers in that country (and perhaps all others) have had finding a receptive audience even within the more confined spaces of gay letters or erotica. The erasure of lesbian literature runs parallel to that of women's literature in general.

I would like to dedicate this volume to the Latinas in higher education–lesbian or otherwise–who are, in many cases, the first in their families to go to college, and who, for the most part, have surmounted incredible obstacles to educate themselves and better their lives. May they become the role models they seek.

Illustration by Jennifer Whiting

Latina Lesbian Writers and Performers:
An Overview

María Dolores Costa

SUMMARY. This article introduces the most significant contemporary Latina lesbian writers and performers in the United States, Latin America, and Spain, giving us a panoramic view of the Latina lesbian canon of the late twentieth and early twenty-first centuries. *[Article copies available for a fee from The Haworth Document Delivery Service: 1-800-HAWORTH. E-mail address: <docdelivery@haworthpress.com> Website: <http://www.HaworthPress. com> © 2003 by The Haworth Press, Inc. All rights reserved.]*

KEYWORDS. Latina lesbian authors, Latina lesbian artists/performers

In the past two decades, we have witnessed the powerful emergence of Latina lesbian literature, art, and thought on the cultural scene in the United

---

María Dolores Costa is Professor of Spanish at California State University, Los Angeles. She received her PhD from the University of Massachusetts, Amherst, and her BA and MA from Kent State University. She specializes in nineteenth and twentieth century literature, and is especially interested in lesbian studies, feminism, nature in literature, and film.

Address correspondence to: María Dolores Costa, 274 West Radcliffe Dr., Claremont, CA 91711.

[Haworth co-indexing entry note]: "Latina Lesbian Writers and Performers: An Overview." Costa, María Dolores. Co-published simultaneously in *Journal of Lesbian Studies* (Harrington Park Press, an imprint of The Haworth Press, Inc.) Vol. 7, No. 3, 2003, pp. 5-26; and: *Latina Lesbian Writers and Artists* (ed: María Dolores Costa) Harrington Park Press, an imprint of The Haworth Press, Inc., 2003. pp. 5-26. Single or multiple copies of this article are available for a fee from The Haworth Document Delivery Service [1-800-HAWORTH, 9:00 a.m. - 5:00 p.m. (EST). E-mail address: docdelivery@haworthpress.com].

10.1300/J155v07n03_02

States and in many Spanish-speaking countries. The creative work that has materialized is diverse and multifaceted–so much so that it is difficult, if not impossible, to lump them all together, except insomuch as they are all the products of Latina lesbians. Even with this, we run into the predicament of defining the terms Latina and lesbian, as these are notoriously problematic designations. For my part, I use the word Latina because it is the generally preferred term today, although it might be less technically correct than the term Hispanic for the group I am discussing: that is, I will refer to women culturally identified with Spanish-speaking countries and groups.[1] I incorporate in my summary women from Spain, from the Spanish-speaking countries of Latin America, and Latina women from the United States who predominantly write and perform in English or who freely mix English and Spanish in their writings and performances. I am including Chicanas under my designation, recognizing that many Chicanas do not choose to classify themselves as Hispanic or Latina.

I use this terminology fully cognizant of the pitfalls of fuzzy ethnic labeling. Millions of disparate women cannot be made to line up meaningfully behind a single word, be it Latina, Hispanic, or whatever the expression of choice. My operating assumption is simply that the women I am discussing here do not inevitably have more in common than a cultural connection (perhaps several generations removed) to a predominantly Spanish-speaking country and a self-defined or outwardly attributed lesbian orientation.

The term lesbian is complicated for different reasons. In some cases, the women I mention here are self-identified or have been so generally identified as lesbians that there is no perceivable conflict. There is, however, some reticence still, especially in the majority Spanish-speaking countries, to be identified with the label of "lesbian writer" or "lesbian performer." It may be that I (following the cue of others) am erroneously attributing a lesbian orientation to some of these women. It is undoubtedly the case, however, that an individual's sexual orientation is less a factor in determining whether or not she has contributed to the body of lesbian writing and art than whether or not her work contributes to a raising of consciousness on lesbian issues.

Here, then, I offer my brief synopsis of Latina lesbian arts and letters today. While I hope that my list includes the more prominent, innovative and/or intriguing authors and performers that have shaped the corpus of contemporary Latina lesbian arts and letters, I recognize that this cannot be an exhaustive inventory. New Latina lesbian writers and artists are cropping up on the cultural scene continually and, on the whole, have shown themselves to be quite prolific. I will not have space to discuss in detail all works by the women cited here. This is simply proposed as a feasible introduction to this field, a brief sampling of the Latina lesbian talent presently available to us. In order to avoid a hierarchical rendering, I have chosen to present the authors and performers in alphabetical order by last name.

I begin with *Magaly Alabau*, a Cuban writer who resides in the U.S. In her work, Alabau deals with lesbian eroticism in a frank, rebellious way. She is the author of *La extremaunción diaria, poemas*[2] and *Electra, Clitemnestra*.[3]

Gloria Anzaldúa is a crucial figure in Chicana/o literature–and, more specifically, in Chicana lesbian literature–as she is arguably the most prominent Chicana lesbian writer today. Besides writing, she has taught Chicano Studies, Feminist Studies, and creative writing at several universities. She has also served as coeditor of *Signs*, a respected feminist publication. Anzaldúa's literary production has been recognized with several honors, including the NEA Fiction Award, the Lesbian Rights Award, and the Sappho Award of Distinction. In her work, Anzaldúa develops feminist and cultural theories, concentrating principally on Chicanos and lesbians and their interactions with the Anglo-American and heterosexual worlds. She relentlessly uncovers the powerful mix of gender, race, culture, class, and sexual orientation within and among individuals. Cultural and family ties play an important role in Anzaldúa's discussions. Her trademark prose is a very personalized and poetic form of the essay that combines English and Spanish, remembrances, historical investigation, and poetry.

Borderlands/La Frontera: The New Mestiza[4] is unquestionably her most important work, and now a classic of U.S. literature. Here Anzaldúa, a native of Texas, speaks of the borderlands as an essential component and creator of an identity that is necessarily multiple and many-sided. The author concludes that Chicanas (lesbian or otherwise) have a critical role to play in the healing of society because they are exceptionally marked by difference, or the intersection of cultures.

Anzaldúa has also edited several notable anthologies. *Making Face, Making Soul/Haciendo Caras: Creative and Critical Perspectives by Women of Color*[5] was the winner of the Lambda Literary Best Small Press Book award. This book, like all those bearing Anzaldúa's name on the cover, investigates such themes as bigotry, sexism, and the cultural roles and identities of women of color. The face referenced in the title is the construction of our identities as women.

This Bridge Called My Back: Writings by Radical Women of Color[6] was coedited by Anzaldúa and Cherríe Moraga (another central personage in Chicana letters). The renowned tome is a collection of essays, poems, and short stories by radical women of color, and is pioneering in that it is the first anthology of this nature. Indeed, a theme addressed in this book and others by Anzaldúa is "white" feminists' silencing and ignorance of their nonwhite, non-Anglo sisters. *This Bridge Called My Back* received the Before Columbus

Foundation American Book Award and has enjoyed a broad readership since its publication.

Azúcar y Crema (Sugar and Cream) is a seven woman Afro-Cuban jazz band that has been profiled in the anthology *Hot Licks: Lesbian Musicians of Note*.[7] They have performed at the celebrated Michigan Womyn's Music Festival in Oceana County.

Marta Balletbò-Coll and *Ana Simón Cerezo*, two Spaniards involved in the film industry, are co-authors of the novel *Hotel Kempinsky*.[8] Originally written in Catalan, this book is a romantic comedy that highlights the world of filmmaking, taking the reader through three European cities–Barcelona, Madrid, and Berlin. Other works bearing Balletbò's signature are the film and book *Costa Brava*.[9]

Diana Bellesi is a lesbian poet from Argentina and the author of *Eroica*,[10] a book of erotic poetry.

Marina Castañeda is the author of *La experiencia homosexual: Para comprender la homosexualidad desde dentro y desde fuera*,[11] which was published in Mexico. In this book, Castañeda discusses the central role of sexual orientation in any discussion of civil rights. Homosexuality, she argues, must be understood in order to arrive at the concepts of individual freedom, tolerance, and pluralism. It is perilous, therefore, to leave this discussion in the hands of the clergy, the judicial system, or the medical community, because it is too significant and eventually affects everyone equally. Castañeda appreciates gay militancy and wants to add her research to the effort for the sake of gays and lesbians, their families, and society as a whole. In stating her purpose, the author notes the paucity of published research in Spanish on this topic.

Born in Argentina in 1963, *Flavia Company* has lived in Spain since the age of ten. She has written several novels and literary critiques, as well as translations of works by others. She also writes a weekly column for the newspaper *El Periódico de Cataluña*. Company publishes in both in Spanish and Catalan. *Dame placer*[12] is her novel about the progressive collapse of a relationship between two women. The book carries a powerful emotional charge, as the protagonist goes through a profound emotional crisis and is ultimately driven to self-destruction when she faces her partner's abandonment. *Melalcor*[13] is a more recent novel by Company.

In her home country of Argentina, *Susana Cook* studied drama and began performing with a small company during the military dictatorship. In 1993, the artist moved to New York City, where she currently resides. This lesbian writer, director, and performer describes herself as a butch lesbian performance artist. She produces and writes her own shows, and has also performed and taught workshops at several universities around the country.

Cook's work deals with political and cultural identities, the body (with all its functions and taboos intact), and sexuality (sexual politics, orientation, etc.). Her productions include *Gross National Product, Hamletango, Spic for Export* and *Tango Lesbiango*[14]–titles that indicate a keen concern with the playful possibilities of language. *Spic for Export* deals with the Hispanic immigrant woman whose labor forms the unrecognized backbone of the United States. *Hamletango*, a recent production, mocks classic culture as being overly straight, white, and upper-class. In this unique adaptation of Shakespeare, the protagonist is a working-class butch prince.

Cook's writing is poignant and darkly humorous. In her "resume," for example, she sardonically pokes fun at U.S. capitalist culture and the victims it creates within the system as she points out her "qualifications" for an unspecified job:

> I like to work with people and without people
> ...
> I can work under pressure, even harassment
> I can work hungry, tired, over time, over you
> I am deeply satisfied to live in America
> I would be happy here
> I am happy already thinking of how happy I would be to work here
> This place is great; I match with the walls
> ...
> I have a corporate soul
> I like this team feeling
> I can easily be pressured into conformity and obedience
> I can pass as nobody
> I can accept very graciously being excluded from opportunities, culture, public debate and power
>
> –So you give jobs? That's very nice of you. You'll give me the possibility to work for the minimum legally possible pay. I am healthy now, but I would get psychosomatic diseases here. I forgot to mention in my resume, I like to go to people's houses and steal their CDs.[15]

Lucía Etxebarría, a young Spanish writer, has already published several books, and many of these have been translated into other European languages. *Beatriz y los cuerpos celestes*[16] was the winner of the Spanish Nadal Prize–an award given to first-time novelists–in 1998. This is a novel about surviving love that features three principal characters: Cat, the lesbian, Mónica, and the Beatriz of the title. *Amor, curiosidad, prozac y dudas*[17] is a novel about the relationship of three women with the love, curiosity, Prozac, and doubts mentioned in the title as they each struggle to make a better life for themselves.[18] *Nosotras que no somos como las demás*[19] is a novel in which Etxebarría critiques the feminine roles assigned to women in late capitalist societies. The book recounts the stories of four women who search for social, political, sexual, and economic freedom despite the many internal and external forces that threaten to bring them down–passions, work, fear, rivalry, drugs, and alcohol.

Carlota Echalecu Tranchant, another Spanish writer, was born in Madrid. *Los ojos del ciervo*[20] is her first novel and the winner of the Carolina Colorado prize in Spain. The book's protagonist is Laura, a married woman who falls in love with another woman possessing "eyes like a deer."

Kleya Forte-Escamilla (also known as Edna Escamill) is a short story writer and novelist. She is the author of *Daughter of the Mountain*,[21] a bildungsroman set in the Southwest. *Mada*[22] is her erotic novel about a Latina lesbian who fixates on a mystifying German woman, while *The Storyteller with Nike Airs and the Barrio Stories*[23] is a book of short stories. Forte-Escamilla's works are filled with Latina lesbian characters and characteristically mix Spanish and English.

Mabel Galán is a Spanish psychologist and writer who prefers to be classified as a woman writer rather than a lesbian writer. *Desde la otra orilla*[24] is her first novel, although she had previously written poetry and short stories. The novel is situated in Madrid and has a protagonist named Alicia who confronts discrimination. Among the many themes presented in the novel, which was critically well received, are lesbianism, immigration, and the Internet as a means for human communication and relationship.[25]

Alicia Gaspar de Alba is a professor and author. *Sor Juana's Second Dream*[26] is her historical novel about the illustrious seventeenth century Mexican writer, Sor Juana Inés de la Cruz (1648-1695), presumed by many to have been a lesbian because of the passionate love poems she addressed to her benefactress–Doña Leonor Carreto, Marquesa de Mancera–and her scathing critique of male abuse of power against women. Gaspar de Alba's book is an intimate portrait of Juana Inés–an illegitimate, self-taught criolla who was born Juana Ramírez de Asbaje–in which she appears as a sensual, strong-willed, intelligent, emotional woman. The novel combines Sor Juana's words, recent scholarship on the poet, and imaginative fiction. Gaspar de Alba is also the author of the essay "Tortillerismo: Work by Chicana Lesbians,"[27] in which she discusses the marginalization of Chicana lesbian writers. Other works by Gaspar de Alba include *The Mystery of Survival and Other Stories*,[28] "Juana Inés,"[29] and "Excerpts from the Sapphic Diary of Sor Juana Inés de la Cruz."[30] With María Herrera Sobek and Demetria Martínez, Gaspar de Alba wrote *Three Times a Woman: Chicana Poetry*.[31]

Ellen M. Gil-Gómez is the author of *Performing La Mestiza: Textual Representations of Lesbians of Color and the Negotiation of Identities*,[32] a book which explores the constructions of ethnicity, gender, and queer identities in the texts of contemporary U.S. lesbians of color. The author leans on theories developed by Gloria Anzaldúa and Judith Butler in her explorations of these works, which were written by African American, Native American, and Asian American women, as well as Latinas.

Marga Gómez is lesbian writer and performer of Cuban and Puerto Rican origins. Born in Harlem, Gómez has lived in San Francisco and Brooklyn. Her parents, using the stage names Willie Chevalier (a Cuban with the given name of Wildredo Gómez) and Margo la Exótica (really Puerto Rican born Margarita Estremera), were also performers. Their variety shows could be seen in U.S. Latin clubs in the 1950s and '60s.

Marga, a recipient of Theater LA's Ovation Award, has had several solo shows. *Memory Tricks,* her solo show from 1993, is a piece about her mother, who led a colorful life, marrying twice and escaping the ennui of her second marriage by fleeing to France, only to return to the United States a confused victim of Alzheimer's. Gómez explored her relationship with her father in the performance piece *A Line Around the Block. Live and Undead,* a comedy, was performed at the Latina Theater Festival in Los Angeles in October 2000. Other solo shows include *Marga Gomez Is Pretty, Witty & Gay, jaywalker,* and *The Twelve Days of Cochina.* In 2002, Gómez performed alongside Carmelita Tropicana in *Single Wet Female,* a show that was billed as a low budget thriller. The artist also starred in *Miss Clairol,* an independent film directed by Melissa Howden, and *Sphere,* a science fiction film directed by Barry Levinson. She has appeared on HBO's *Comic Relief,* on Comedy Central's *Out There,* and on Tracy Ullman's variety show on HBO. Gómez has an audio CD, *Hung Like a Fly,*[33] and excerpts from some of her shows can be read in *Contemporary Plays by Women of Color.*[34]

Irene González Frei is the pseudonym of an author who has chosen to remain anonymous–in the closet, as it were. González Frei is the author of the novel *Tu nombre escrito en el agua,*[35] an erotic fantasy about Sofía, a young woman from Madrid, who develops a passionate relationship with a woman named Marina. The novel won the Sonrisa Vertical (Vertical Smile) prize in 1995–this being an award given annually to what is deemed the best erotic novel.

Psychologist and psychotherapist *Susana Guzner* was born in 1944 in Argentina. She left that country following the rape, torture, and murder of her only sister at the hands of the death squads and has been living in Spain since 1976. Currently she resides in the Canary Islands. *La insensata geometría del amor*[36] is her first novel. This is a lesbian love thriller with a protagonist/narrator named María, a translator who falls in love with a woman named Eva whom she meets in an airport. Eva is an enigmatic figure with a hidden past. In fact, part of the intrigue in the novel revolves around Eva's true identity. There are numerous cultural references interwoven throughout the work, beginning with the names of the two principal characters, who represent the two culturally constructed poles of womanhood in the Catholic mind: Mary, the good and Eve, the wicked. The title of the novel alludes ironically to the complicated web of perceptions in human relationships: that is, there are no precise geometric shapes when humans interact and fall in love. The novel has proven to be quite popular with readers and has been very well received in critical circles. Guzner has also written television screenplays, some plays, and opinion pieces, along with texts in the field of psychology. Women are always the focal point of her creative writing.

Mili Hernández is not really a writer or performer, but she deserves a mention for her contributions to Latina lesbian letters. Hernández is a political activist who appears regularly in the Spanish media as a spokesperson for gay and lesbian issues. She and her partner hold the distinction of being the first lesbian couple to officially register in Madrid as domestic partners. Hernández is also credited with taking the rainbow flag to Spain. With Arnaldo Gancedo, she founded Berkana, Spain's first gay and lesbian bookstore, in Madrid's gay district. For a while, she edited a lesbian magazine, *Nosotras* (Us). In order to foment gay and lesbian literature in Spain she–along with Cómplices, a Barcelona gay and lesbian bookstore–began Egales (Editorial Gay y Lesbiana), the first Spanish gay and lesbian press. While there are now more independent queer presses in Spain, Egales has been one of the most successful in publishing and distributing works by Spanish lesbian and gay male authors.

Writer and journalist *María Felicitas Jaime* was born in Buenos Aires, Argentina. In her homeland, Jaime has worked as a television screen writer and a radio news editor. She has published short stories and books, as well as articles in magazines. Jaime is a militant feminist who champions Latin American women and gays and lesbians in her work. As she confronts injustice and the abuse of power, she has made her share of enemies along the way. In the 1980s, presumably because of Argentina's economic crisis, Jaime decided to write erotic pulp fiction for a lesbian audience. *Pasiones*[37] is a humorous novel situated in an imaginary world without bigotry, where everyone is free and all respect each other.

Sara Levi Calderón is a Mexican writer and the author of *The Two Mujeres*,[38] an extremely popular novel. The work is a bildungsroman that investigates issues of social class, gender roles, and religion. The protagonist is a woman from a wealthy Jewish family living in Mexico City. Although married, she falls in love with another woman, and eventually leaves her conventional life, ignoring pressures from her family, in order to be with her lover.

Aurora Levins Morales is a teacher, historian, and writer of Jewish and Puerto Rican descent. Themes in her writings include anti-Semitism, classism, feminism, multicultural history, and racism. Levins Morales is the author of *Getting Home Alive*,[39] *Medicine Stories: History, Culture and the Politics of Integrity*,[40] and *Remedios: Stories of Earth and Iron from the History of Puertorriqueñas*.[41] This last work is a history of the extraordinary women of the many cultures that have come into contact on the Puerto Rican island. Through stories of female activists from different groups, Levins Morales weaves the identity of the contemporary Puerto Rican woman.

Erika López is a New Jersey born writer, cartoonist (for the *San Francisco Bay Times*), and spoken word performer. Her books are all partially based on autobiographical material. Like her recurring character, Tomato Rodriguez, she describes herself as a half Puerto Rican, Quaker, bisexual biker-chick. López has a feisty, shocking sense of humor that some have found offensive (as was no doubt intended). In her work there is much sardonic commentary on political and social themes, along with references to both highbrow and garish elements of popular culture. *Lap Dancing for Mommy*,[42] *Flaming Iguanas*,[43] and *They Call Me Mad Dog*[44] are three of her titles.

Elena Martínez is the author of *Lesbian Voices from Latin America: Breaking Ground*,[45] a work of literary history and criticism. In this volume, Martínez analyzes common themes and motifs in the works of Latin American lesbian writers of the twentieth century, concentrating on texts that privilege a lesbian point of view. While not all-encompassing in its scope, the book is a significant contribution to the study of Latin American lesbian writing.

Catalan writer *Ana María Moix,* the sister of well known gay writer Terenci Moix, is primarily known as a poet. Her literary career began in the late 1960s. In 1970 she published her first novel, *Julia*,[46] the story of an adolescent girl's first love–her English teacher.

Argentine critic, novelist, and short story writer *Sylvia Molloy* lives in the U.S. She has written several literary critiques of gay and lesbian themes in Hispanic letters, including works on Teresa de la Parra[47] and Alejandra Pizarnik.[48] Together with Robert McKee Irwin, she edited the book *Hispanisms and Homosexualities*,[49] a work which brings together queer studies and Hispanic cultural studies, using each to illuminate the other. Sara Castro-Klaren and Beatriz Sarlo were Molloy's co-editors on the volume *Women's Writing in Latin America: An Anthology*.[50] Molloy is also the author of the narrative work *En breve cárcel*.[51]

Norma Mogrovejo is a Peruvian lesbian living in Mexico. Mogrovejo has written from a historical perspective on the feminist and lesbian movements in

Latin America. She has several books and articles on the subject of lesbianism in Latin America to her credit, including *El amor is bxh/2. Una propuesta de análisis histórico-metodológica del movimiento lésbico y sus amores con los movimientos homosexual y feminista en América Latina*[52] and *Un amor que se atrevió a decir su nombre: La lucha de las lesbianas y su relación con los movimientos homosexual y feminista en América Latina.*[53] This last work is a history and analysis of the Latin American lesbian movement, especially in relation to the feminist movement and the gay rights movement. Perhaps not surprisingly, Mogrovejo finds many similarities in these three movements as they have acted in Latin American societies, although the heterosexism of the feminist movement and the misogyny and androcentrism of the gay rights movement eventually take their toll on the solidarity Latin American lesbians have found with gay males and straight women. The researcher uses case studies from Mexico, Argentina, Peru, Chile, Costa Rica, Nicaragua, and Brazil in her effort to construct a collective Latina American lesbian identity. Mogrovejo is also the author of the piece "The Lesbian Movement in Latin America: A Herstory,"[54] a concise summary of the development of lesbian consciousness in Latin America. *Lestimonios: Voces de mujeres lesbianas 1950-2000*[55] retells the quotidian lesbian history of the last fifty years of the twentieth century using stories, testimonies and poetry.

As mentioned earlier, *Cherríe Moraga* is an eminent Chicana (or, more precisely, the daughter of a Mexican mother and an Anglo father) lesbian writer. A native of Whittier, California, Moraga has worked as a high school teacher in Los Angeles. In 1977 she moved to San Francisco to pursue her writing career and to be open about her lesbianism. She is currently teaching at Stanford University in California. Moraga writes poems, short stories, and essays on Chicana culture and sexuality. An important aspect of Moraga's work is authenticity–that is, writing with her own voice as a lesbian woman of color. *Loving in the War Years: Lo que nunca pasó por sus labios*[56] is a book of poetry and essays of a testimonial nature. Many of the entries in this work relate to the topic of being a lesbian in a Chicano family. Indeed, *Loving in the War Years* was one of the first books published in the United States to have a Chicana lesbian perspective. Other works include *Cuentos: Stories by Latinas,*[57] a work Moraga edited along with Alma Gómez and Mariana Romo-Carmona, and *Giving Up the Ghost.*[58] Several years later, Moraga edited *The Sexuality of Latinas*[59] along with Norma Alarcón and Ana Castillo. In *The Last Generation: Prose and Poetry*[60] Moraga again explores themes of conflict between Chicana lesbians and their families. *Waiting in the Wings: Portrait of a Queer Motherhood*[61] recounts Moraga's personal experiences as the mother of a two-pound baby boy struggling to survive. Her partner, her family, and the child's father play a significant role in these experiences.

Watsonville/a Circle in the Dirt[62] is a recent political play penned by Moraga. In addition to her writing, Moraga founded and directed DramaDivas, a writing-for-performance workshop for queer youth of color.

Illy Nes is a young Spanish woman (born in 1973) with a passion for literature and painting who writes for the literary magazine *Catarsis*. Nes was granted the Bigayles prize for lesbian narrative in the year 2000, an award given by the Asociación de Gais y Lesbianas de L'Hospitalet. As a fiction writer, Nes writes candidly about sexuality. *Ámame*[63] is a novel centered on Gina Molins, a Catalan lawyer who eventually becomes embroiled in a lesbian love triangle. Nes has proven to be popular with Spanish-speaking lesbian readers.

Spanish writer *Carmen Nestares* is the author of *Venus en Buenos Aires*,[64] a novel revolving around an Internet relationship that develops between a Spanish woman and an Argentine woman. This pulp fiction work delves into homophobia among Argentines and Spaniards.

Cuban born exile *Achy Obejas* makes her home in Chicago. This fiction writer and journalist has also published poetry and has worked as a cultural critic for the *Chicago Tribune*. Family ties play an important role in Obejas' fiction. Much of her work is about lesbians living in tight-knit Latino communities and Cuban families. *We Came All the Way from Cuba So You Could Dress Like This?*[65] is a collection of humorous short stories written from various perspectives, including that of lesbians, gay men, immigrants, and people suffering from AIDS. *Memory Mambo*[66] is Obejas' novel about a young Cuban lesbian named Juani who is exiled to the United States with her family. *Days of Awe*[67] follows the fictional life of Alejandra San José, who was born in Havana on New Year's Day, 1959, just as Fidel Castro was coming to power in Cuba. Like her author, Alejandra comes to the United States with her family and settles in Chicago. As an interpreter, she eventually returns to Cuba, where she investigates her own past and discovers for the first time that her family was of Jewish origin.

Los Angeles native *Sheila Ortiz Taylor* is a Chicana novelist, poet, and professor. Her 1982 work *Faultline*[68] is perhaps one of the first novels to feature a Chicana lesbian character. *Imaginary Parents: A Family Autobiography*[69] is a memoir that portrays a bicultural family in Southern California. *Coachella*,[70] as the title suggests, is a work of fiction set in the Coachella Valley.

Mónica Palacios is a queer Chicana writer and performance artist who resides in California. In her performances, she comments humorously on gender roles, sexuality, and the concept of normality. Palacios wrote *Clock*, a play about a lesbian couple trying to decide whether or not to have a baby, and *Bésame mucho*, a comedic performance that formed part of the Latina Theater Festival in Los Angeles (October 2000).

Terri de la Peña burst on to the literary scene with *Margins*,[71] a coming of age story with a Chicana lesbian protagonist who confronts racism, sexism, and homophobia. This was followed by *Latin Satins*,[72] a novel that centers on the music scene in Santa Monica and the Mexican roots of this West Coast city where the author resides, and later, *Faults: A Novel*,[73] which describes the lives of three generations of Chicana women. The Chicana author has written many essays and book reviews for publications like *Lesbian News* and *Lambda Book Report*. Her work has also been published in several collections, including *Dyke Life*[74] and *Lesbian Friendships*.[75]

Chicana historian *Emma Pérez* has theorized on the Chicano/a Diaspora. In *The Decolonial Imaginary: Writing Chicanas into History*,[76] Pérez defines "third space feminism" as it has played out in the lives of Mexican women throughout the twentieth century. Her objective is to assemble a new Chicana feminist history. The "decolonial imaginary" of the title is the space between the colonial past and the postcolonial future. With *Gulf Dreams*,[77] Pérez ventured into the realm of fiction. Written in a dream diary format, *Gulf Dreams* is a coming of age story told from the perspective of a Chicana lesbian and set in a Gulf Coast Texas town inconspicuously named El Pueblo.

Cristina Peri Rossi is an illustrious poet and novelist from Uruguay who lives in Spain. Lesbianism and writing are intertwined themes in Peri Rossi's work. For her, lesbianism is a form of feminism, as is writing itself—although she does argue against reductive theories that attempt to define a certain form of writing as "lesbian writing." Some critics view her work as lesbian pornography because she deals so explicitly with eroticism between women. Erotic passion and the frustration that ensues from not being able to unite wholly with the loved one are common themes in Peri Rossi's work. Among the many titles bearing her name we find *A Forbidden Passion: Stories*[78] and *Evohe*.[79]

Inmaculada Perpetusa-Seva, an assistant professor of Spanish, and *Lourdes Torres*, an associate professor of Latin American/Latino studies, are the editors of the volume *Tortilleras: Hispanic and U.S. Latina Lesbian Expression*,[80] a forthcoming anthology of queer readings of Latin American, Spanish, and U.S. Latina literature and culture that covers many different writers and performers.

Galician writer *María-Xosé Queizán* has written essays, plays, poetry, and novels. She began her writing career with *El Pueblo Gallego*, a newspaper in her native city, Vigo. While in her twenties, Queizán got involved with theater, and from 1967 to 1968 she directed the group Teatro Popular Galego (Popular Galician Theater), which she founded. In the early seventies, Queizán went to live for a spell in Paris, where she became acquainted with the contemporary French novel. Upon returning to Galicia, she began to study Galician philology at the University of Santiago de Compostela. This former high school teacher of Galician language and literature frequently writes in her native language as a form of political resistance to Castilian[81] supremacy.

Queizán is a staunch feminist who has written extensively on the situation of women in her native region of Spain, frequently tying the political, social, and economic control over women to that which Galicia has suffered. Her works are numerous and include *A muller en Galicia*,[82] a feminist essay; *A semellanza*,[83] a novel that deals with gay life in contemporary Spain; *Amantia*,[84] a work of historical fiction that tells the story of fourth-century Galician women involved in a movement against the misogynist, orthodox Christianity imposed by the Roman empire; a collection of poetry called *Despertar das amantes*;[85] *Misoxinia e racismo na poesía de Pondal*,[86] an essay about the work of popular Galician nationalist poet Eduardo Pondal, and *¡Sentinela, alerta!*,[87] Queizán's first venture into the short story genre. The ten stories collected in this last work are unified by their being situated in the space of prisons during the Franco dictatorship and presenting the violence, corruption, cruelty, and desolation that was prison life at the time. The stories relate the darkest aspects of human nature, such as the torture and degradation of women, gays, and other less fortunate members of society.

Juanita Ramos' 1987 compilation, *Compañeras: Latina Lesbians*,[88] is a groundbreaking work. This anthology, edited by Ramos, collects the oral histories, fiction, poetry, essays, and art of numerous Latina lesbians who live in the United States. The Latina Lesbian History Project, which published the work, was founded precisely because other presses would not commit to publishing and distributing this bilingual work.

Bessy Reina, a Cuban-Panamanian poet, has had her work published in several anthologies. Reina has also edited the culture/arts section of *El Extra News*, a Connecticut bilingual newspaper.

Reno is a Latina lesbian comedian who goes by one name and who recently gained notoriety for being one of the first (perhaps *the* first) comedians in the U.S. to attempt to find humor related to the events of September 11, 2001. This she did in her show, *Rebel Without a Pause*, which debuted one month after the tragic events in New York City, home to Reno. The show is a mix of memoir and political satire in which Reno wittily derides the limited thinking and frenzied patriotism George W. Bush, Donald Rumsfeld, and John Ashcroft attempted to instill in the aftermath of the attack. Reno's film, *Reno Finds Her Mom*,[89] is a documentary about her attempt to find the birth mother who gave her up for adoption.

Aleida Rodríguez, a Cuban-American poet currently residing in Los Angeles, has come out with *Garden of Exile: Poems*,[90] her first published collection. This winner of the 1998 Kathryn A. Morton Prize in Poetry has been critically well received. Rodríguez, who mixes Spanish and English in her writing, uses the enigmatic power of language and words as a theme in her work. "I'd like to explain/how difficult it is to work with words," she proclaims in the poem "Plein Air" (34). Other poems are autobiographical, dealing with her identity as a Cuban immigrant to the United States and as a lesbian.

Rosamaría Roffiel, a native of Veracruz, Mexico, is a self-taught journalist and writer. Roffiel worked for over ten years with the newspaper *Excelsior*, then with the magazines *Proceso* and *Fem*,[91] always dealing openly with lesbian identity and lesbian community in her work. Her book *Amora*[92] is credited with being the first lesbian novel published in Mexico–that is, the first novel which openly discusses lesbianism and places it in the foreground. Roffiel has also published a testimonio and some poetry.

Born in Chile, *Mariana Romo-Carmona* has been living in the United States since 1966. She is one of the first members of Kitchen Table: Women of Color Press and a co-founder of the Latina Lesbian History Project. Her works include "Latina Lesbians,"[93] *Conversaciones: relatos de padres y madres de hijas lesbianas e hijos gay*,[94] "The Patlatonalli Manifesto: Latin American Lesbians as Sociopolitical Leaders,"[95] *Living at Night*,[96] a novel about a working-class Puerto Rican lesbian, and *Speaking Like an Immigrant*,[97] a collection of short stories about different people making a way in a new culture.

Mexican writer *Gilda Salinas* has published short stories, a novel, and plays, several of which have been performed in Mexico and Los Angeles.

The very colorful *Tatiana de la Tierra* was born in Colombia and came to live in Miami when she was a young girl. She is a short story writer and essayist who has written chapters for anthologies and articles. In the 1990s, she began publishing *Esto no tiene nombre*,[98] a Latina lesbian quarterly magazine that later became *Conmoción*. The periodical has been a bilingual publication under both names, and has provided a forum for the works of numerous Latina lesbian writers, publishing pieces on such notables as Cherríe Moraga, Achy Obejas, Carmelita Tropicana, and Luz María Umpierre, to name a few.

In highly personal articles, Tatiana reports on the happenings in Latina lesbian literature and the arts–noteworthy magazines, new publications, group activities, etc.–with a humorous, defiant mix of Spanish and English. In her online newsletter, *La Telaraña*, she self-reports, "estoy escribiendo academic & creative cosas full of myself & growing gray hairs, sometimes feeling condenada & other times fortunate."[99]

Alina Troyano is more famously known by her stage name of *Carmelita Tropicana*. This artist, of Cuban origin, is noteworthy for her highly political humorous work. *Milk of Amnesia–Leche de Amnesia*[100] is a self-written performance piece in which Carmelita Tropicana transmits the story of a Cuban-American lesbian's trip back to her mother island. "El Recibo Social" and

"Speech at the LUST Conference" appear in *The New Fuck You: Adventures in Lesbian Reading*.[101] The book *I, Carmelita Tropicana: Performing Between Cultures*[102] includes her plays *Chicas 2000, The Conquest of Mexico as Seen Through the Eyes of Hernan Cortez's Horse*, and *Milk of Amnesia*. Ela Troyano made a film featuring Carmelita Tropicana's monologues and performances. Carmelita and Ela collaborated on the screenplay for this film, *Carmelita Tropicana: Your Kunst Is Your Waffen*,[103] which narrates a day in the life of the single lesbian character. Enhanced with telenovela-inspired melodrama, musical interludes, and Carmelita Tropicana's outrageous sense of humor, the film won a Teddy Bear award for best short film at the Berlin Film Festival.

Carla Trujillo is best known as the editor of *Chicana Lesbians: The Girls Our Mothers Warned Us About*,[104] an anthology of poetry, essays, fiction, and artwork that includes pieces by many of the Chicanas listed here (such as Moraga, Palacios and Anzaldúa). Trujillo's later anthology, *Living Chicana Theory*,[105] brought together Chicana feminist theorists from several disciplines–again counting several of the women listed here (Anzaldúa, Gaspar de Alba, Emma Pérez, Yarbro-Bejarano, and Trujillo herself). In her own essay in this volume, "La Virgen de Guadalupe and Her Reconstruction in Chicana Lesbian Desire," Trujillo argues that Chicana lesbians can repossess the popular (though heterosexist) image of the Mexican Virgin as their own.

The Spanish feminist writer *Esther Tusquets* is recognized in Spain principally as the director of the Spanish publishing house, Lumen. Although she is not one to publicly identify herself as a lesbian, she is generally credited with opening Spanish literature to lesbian themes with her trilogy (which has been translated into English): *El mismo mar de todos los veranos*,[106] *El amor es un juego solitario*,[107] and *Varada tras el último naufragio*.[108] The first work of the trilogy, published when Tusquets was forty-two, relates the story of a brief lesbian relationship between two very different women–a middle-aged narrator and her devoted, naive Latin American student–who are caught in the middling, deceitful milieu of the Catalan bourgeoisie. The next two books in the trilogy, along with later works by Tusquets, also incorporate lesbian themes. *Correspondencia privada*,[109] the novelist's latest work, mixes reality and fantasy through letters written by the protagonist to several characters she has loved throughout the years. In her letters, she reflects not only her own personal feelings and growth, but political and social developments in Spain from the civil war to just shortly before the death of Franco. Tusquets' prose is marked by her lyrical, stylish, nuanced prose, sensual imagery, and her distinct expressions of female sexuality.

Puerto Rican scholar and poet *Luz María Umpierre* has been living on the U.S. mainland since 1974. Umpierre writes erotic poetry and explores issues of femininity and lesbianism in her prose. She has also spoken out about the issue of homophobia in academia.

Lola Van Guardia is the quaint pseudonym of Isabel Franc, a teacher from Barcelona who works with deaf children. Originally Lola Van Guardia was to be a character in the novel *Franc* and was to write a novelized soap opera, but soon became the "author" of a series of books notorious for their erotic content. *Con pedigree*[110] is a Van Guardia novel of intrigue set in the Barcelona lesbian bar scene and the first novel in an unplanned trilogy.[111] It was followed by *Plumas de doble filo*,[112] an entertaining novel populated with lesbians, and *La mansión de las tríbadas*.[113] The series contains much humor, romance, and mystery. Isabel Franc has also published an erotic novel under her given name: *Entre todas las mujeres*,[114] a scandalous parody of erotic mysticism in which a woman, as counseled by her Opus Dei psychotherapist, literally falls in love with the Virgin Mary. The novel won the 1992 Sonrisa Vertical award in Spain.

Chabela Vargas (Isabel Vargas Lizano) is a singer of popular Mexican and Latin American songs, many written by the Mexican composers she helped turn into classics, José Alfredo Jiménez and Agustín Lara. Though generally considered Mexican, Vargas was in fact born in San Joaquín de Flores, Costa Rica. Her true gift, besides her singing voice, is her incomparable personality and her singular perspective on life. Though she has recorded over eighty albums throughout her career, the peak of her success in Mexico came in the first half of the 1960s, when she regularly performed in bohemian clubs. Vargas was an outrageous individual in the Mexican cultural scene because of her self-outing through her performance. In due course, she was faulted for her "obscene" behavior, which included flirting with women in the audience or making a spectacular entrance on a motorcycle. Vargas enjoyed a major comeback in Spain, when she was 74, by recording two albums as she toured the country. Spanish film director Pedro Almodóvar featured Vargas' voice in his films and soon cast her in an on-screen role. In the year 2000, Spain awarded Vargas the Great Cross of Isabel the Catholic. Yvonne Yarbro-Bejarano notes, "In her public lesbian identification and performance style, singer Chabela Vargas creates a space for a U.S. Latina lesbian reading within Mexican and Latin American popular music."[115] Vargas' autobiography, *Y si quieres saber de mi pasado*,[116] recounts the artist's emotional and professional development, including the social scene surrounding Vargas in 1940s-1950s Mexico, which allowed her to encounter such celebrities as Bette Davis, Frida Kahlo, Diego Rivera, and Elizabeth Taylor. In the work, the singer relates that she never intended to make a cause out of her lesbianism, but she never chose to hide it either.

I complete my list with the aforementioned *Yvonne Yarbro-Bejarano*, a literary critic who has written rather extensively on Latina lesbians. She is the author of such works as *Crossing the Border with Chabela Vargas: A Chicana Femme's Tribute*,[117] *De-constructing the Lesbian Body: Cherríe Moraga's Loving in the War Years*,[118] *Expanding the Categories of Race in Lesbian and Gay Studies*,[119] and *The Lesbian Body in Latina Cultural Production*.[120]

To conclude my introduction to Latina lesbian arts and letters, I provide a bibliography of other works (in English and Spanish) that may be of interest to those who wish to explore this area more thoroughly. Once more, I cannot possibly include every work written about the women listed above. I concentrate on more general scholarship: thematic works or works dealing with more than one author.

NOTES

1. The term Latina typically includes women from Portuguese-speaking countries as well, and has sometimes also included Filipinas.
2. Rondas, 1986.
3. Aníbal Pinto, 1986.
4. Spinsters/Aunt Lute, 1987.
5. Aunt Lute, 1990.
6. Persephone Press, 1981.
7. Gynergy Books, 1997.
8. Salir del Armario, 2002. Salir del Armario (Leaving the Closet) is a collection of gay and lesbian themed publications.
9. Naiad Press, 1997.
10. Tierra Firme/Último Reino, 1998.
11. The Homosexual Experience: Understanding Homosexuality Inside and Out. Paidós, 2000.
12. Give Me Pleasure. Emecé, 1999.
13. Muchnik Editores, 2000.
14. This last one is a monthly series on Public Access Cable Television, Manhattan Neighborhood Network.
15. http://www.susanacook.com/resume.htm
16. Beatrice and the Celestial Bodies. Ediciones Destino, 1997.
17. Plaza y Janés, 1997.
18. The book was made into a film that was released in 2000. Etxebarría collaborated on the screenplay with the director, Miguel Santesmases.
19. We Who Are Not Like the Rest. Ediciones Destino, 2000.
20. The Eyes of the Deer. Egales, 1998.
21. Aunt Lute Books, 1991.
22. Sister Vision Press, 1993.
23. Aunt Lute, 1994.
24. From the Other Shore. Odisea, 2001. Odisea is a lesbigay publishing house.

25. Lesbians and gays in Spain are among the most frequent users of the Internet in that country.

26. University of New Mexico Press, 1999.

27. *Signs* 18.4 (Summer 1993): 956-64.

28. Bilingual Press, 1993.

29. In *Growing Up Chicana/o*, William Morrow & Co., 1993.

30. In *Tasting Life Twice: Lesbian Literary Fiction by 7 New American Writers*, Avon Books, 1995.

31. Bilingual Press, 1989.

32. Garland Press, 2000.

33. Uproar Records, 1997.

34. Routledge, 1996.

35. Your Name Written on Water. Tusquets, 1995.

36. Love's Senseless Geometry. Plaza y Janés, 2001.

37. Horas y Horas, 1994.

38. Translated by Gina Kaufer (Aunt Lute, 1991). Originally published as *Dos mujeres* (Diana, 1990).

39. Firebrand, 1986.

40. South End Press, 1998.

41. South End Press, 2001.

42. Seal, 1997.

43. S&S Trade, 1997.

44. Simon and Schuster, 1998.

45. Garland, 1996.

46. Lumen, 1991.

47. A Venezuelan writer (1889-1936).

48. An Argentine writer (1936-1972).

49. Duke University Press, 1998.

50. Westview, 1991.

51. In a Small Prison. Seix Barral, 1981.

52. Love is bxh/2. A Proposal for a Historical-Methodological Analysis of the Lesbian Movement and Its Loves with the Homosexual and Feminist Movements in Latin America. México: Centro de Documentación y Archivo Histórico Lésbico, 1996.

53. A Love that Dared to Speak Its Name: The Lesbian Struggle and Its Relation to the Homosexual and Feminist Movements in Latin America. México: Centro de Documentación y Archivo Histórico Lésbico, 2000.

54. *Lesbian News* 26.2 (September 2000): 52.

55. Lestimonies: Voices of Lesbian Women 1950-2000. Plaza y Valdés, 2001.

56. South End Press, 1983.

57. Kitchen Table, Women of Color Press, 1983.

58. West End Press, 1986.

59. Third Woman Press, 1993.

60. South End Press, 1993.

61. Firebrand Books, 1997.

62. University of New Mexico Press, 2001.

63. Love Me. Salir del Armario, 2002.

64. Odisea Editorial, 2001.

65. Cleis Press, 1994.

66. Cleis Press, 1996.

67. Ballantine Books, 2001.

68. Naiad, 1982.

69. University of New Mexico Press, 1996.

70. University of New Mexico Press, 1998.

71. The Seal Press, 1992.

72. Seal, 1994.

73. Alyson Publications, 1999.

74. Basic Books, 1995.

75. NYU Press, 1996.

76. Indiana University Press, 1999.

77. Third Woman Press, 1996.

78. Cleis Press, 1993.

79. Azul Editions, 1994.

80. Temple University Press, 2003.

81. In Spain, Castilian is the favored term for the language commonly referred to simply as Spanish in the United States.

82. Woman in Galicia. Ediciós do Castro, 1977.

83. Edicións Sotelo Blanco, 1977. Translated into English by Ana M. Spitzmesser as *Likeness* (Peter Lang, 1999).

84. Edicións Xerais de Galicia, 1984.

85. The awakening of the lovers. Espiral Maior, 1991.

86. Misogyny and Racism in the Poetry of Pondal. Laiovento, 1998.

87. Sentinel, Alert! Xerais Narrativa, 2002.

88. Latina Lesbian History Project, 1987.

89. HBO, 1998.

90. Sarbande, 1999.

91. *Fem* has published numerous articles on lesbianism.

92. Planeta Mexicana, 1989.

93. In *A Queer World*; NYU Press, 1997.

94. Conversations: Stories of Fathers and Mothers of Lesbian and Gay Children. Cleis Press, 2001.

95. *GLQ*, 3.4 (1997): 467-80.

96. Spinsters Ink, 1997.

97. Lesbian History Project, 1999.

98. This Has No Name.

99. *La Telaraña* (http://www.indiana.edu/~arenal/tela.html).

100. Included in *O Solo Homo: The New Queer Performance*. Edited by Holly Hughes and David Roman (Grove Press, 1998).

101. Edited by Eileen Myles & Liz Kotz (Semiotext(e), 1995).

102. Edited by Chon A. Noriega (Beacon, 2000).

103. First Run/Icarus Films, 1994.

104. Third Woman Press, 1991.

105. Third Woman Press, 1998.

106. The Same Sea as Every Summer. Editorial Lumen, 1978.

107. Love Is a Solitary Game. Editorial Lumen, 1979.

108. Stranded After the Last Shipwreck. Editorial Lumen, 1980.

109. Anagrama, 2001.

110. With Pedigree. Egales, 1997.

111. The trilogy came about in response to the popularity of the first book.

112. Double-edged Feathers. Egales, 1999.
113. The Mansion of the Tribads. Egales, 2001.
114. Among All Women. Tusquets, 1992.
115. Yarbro-Bejarano, Yvonne, "Crossing the Border with Chabela Vargas: A Chicana Femme's Tribute," *LOLApress* 13 (October 31, 2000): 48.
116. And If You Want to Know About My Past. Aguilar, 2002.
117. In Balderston and Guy, *Sex and Sexuality in Latin America* (NYU Press, 1997).
118. In *The Lesbian and Gay Studies Reader*. Edited by Henry Abelove, Michèle Aina Barale, and David M. Halperin (Routledge, 1993). Also in Trujillo's *Living Chicana Theory*.
119. In *Professions of Desire: Lesbian and Gay Studies in Literature*. Edited by George E. Haggerty and Bonnie Zimmerman (MLA Publications, 1995).
120. In Bergmann and Smith's *¿Entiendes? Queer Readings, Hispanic Writings* (Duke University Press, 1995).

BIBLIOGRAPHY

A las orillas de Lesbos. Narrativa lésbica. Lima: MHOL, 1997.
Aponte-Parés, Luis and Jorge Merced. "Páginas Omitidas: The Gay and Lesbian Presence." In *The Puerto Rican Movement: Voices from the Diaspora*, edited by Andrés Torres and José E. Velázquez. Philadelphia: Temple University Press, 1998.
Arrizón, Alicia and Lillian Manzor, eds. *Latinas on Stage*. Berkeley: Third Woman Press, 2000.
Arrizón, Alicia. *Latina Performance: Traversing the Stage*. Bloomington: Indiana University Press, 1999.
Balderston, Daniel and Donna Guy, eds. *Sex and Sexuality in Latin America*. New York : New York University Press, 1997.
Bergmann, Emile L. and Paul Julian Smith, eds. *¿Entiendes? Queer Readings, Hispanic Writings*. Durham: Duke University Press, 1995.
Castillo-Speed, Lillian, ed. *Latina: Women's Voices from the Borderlands*. New York: Simon and Schuster, 1995.
Castro, María. *El lesbianismo como una cuestión política*. Mexico City: Ponencia, 1987.
Castro-Klaren, Sara, Sylvia Molloy, and Beatriz Sarlo, eds. *Women's Writing in Latin America*. Boulder: Westview Press, 1991.
Chavez-Silverman, Susana & Hernández, Librada, eds. *Reading and Writing the Ambiente: Queer Sexualities in Latino, Latin American, and Spanish Culture*. Madison: University of Wisconsin Press, 2000.
Cortina, Guadalupe. *Invenciones multitudinarias: Escritoras judíomexicanas contemporáneas*. Newark, Del.: Juan de la Cuesta, 2000.
Erro-Peralta, Nora, ed. *Beyond the Border: A New Age in Latin American Women's Fiction*. Gainesville: University Press of Florida, 2000.
Espin, Oliva M. "Issues of Identity in the Psychology of Latina Lesbians." *Lesbian Psychologies*. Ed. Boston Lesbian Psychologies Collective. Urbana: University of Illinois Press, 1987. 35-55.
Ferguson, Ann. "Lesbianism, Feminism and Empowerment in Nicaragua." *Social Review* 21. 3-4 (1991): 75-97.

Foster, David William. *Gay and Lesbian Themes in Latin American Writing*. Austin: University of Texas Press, 1991.

_____. *Latin American Writers on Gay and Lesbian Themes: A Bio-Critical Sourcebook*. Westport, Conn: Greenwood Press; 1994.

_____. "Social Pact and Lesbian Writing." *Literatura Mexicana/Mexican Literature*. Ed. José Miguel Oviedo. Philadelphia: University of Pennsylvania Press, 1993. pp. 92-103.

Flores, Yolanda. *The Drama of Gender: Feminist Theater by Women of the Americas*. New York: Peter Lang, 2000.

Fusková, Ilse and Claudina Marek. *Amor de mujeres: El lesbianismo en la Argentina, hoy*. Buenos Aires: Planeta, 1994.

Fusková-Komreich, Ilse. "Lesbian Activism in Argentina: A Recent But Very Powerful Phenomenon." *The Third Pink Book*. Ed. A. Hendriks, R. Tielman, and E. van der Veen. Buffalo: Prometheus Books, 1993. 82-85.

Galindo, D. Letticia, María Dolores Gonzales, eds. *Speaking Chicana: Voice, Power, and Identity*. Tucson: University of Arizona Press, 1999.

Garza, Luis Alberto de la, comp. *Preliminary Chicano and Latino lesbian and gay bibliography*. Berkeley, CA : Archivos Rodrigo Reyes, 1994.

Geografías de la sexualidad y el lesbianismo. México: Centro de Investigación y Capacitación de la Mujer, 1997.

González, Deena J. "Masquerades: Viewing the New Chicana Lesbian Anthologies." *Out/Look* 15 (1991): 80-83.

Hidalgo, Hilda and Elia Hidalgo-Christensen. "The Puerto Rican Cultural Response to Female Homosexuality." *The Puerto Rican Women*. Ed. Edna Acosta-Belén. New York: Praeger, 1979. 110-23.

_____. "The Puerto Rican Lesbian and the Puerto Rican Community." *Journal of Homosexuality* 2 (1976-1977): 109-21.

Hughes, Holly and David Roman, eds. *O solo homo: The New Queer Performance*. New York: Grove Press, 1998.

Ippolito, Emilia. *Caribbean Women Writers: Identity and Gender*. Columbia: Camden House, 2000.

López-Cabrales, María del Mar. *La pluma y la represión: Escritoras contemporáneas argentinas*. New York: Peter Lang, 1999.

Malavé, Arnaldo Cruz and Martin F. Manalansan, ed. *Queer Globalization: Citizenship and the Afterlife of Colonialism*. New York: New York University Press, 2002.

Marchant, Elizabeth A. *Critical Acts: Latin American Women and Cultural Criticism*. Gainesville: University Press of Florida, 1999.

Marrero, María Teresa. "Out of the Fringe? Out of the Closet: Latina/Latino Theatre and Performance in the 1990s." *TDR: The Drama Review* 44.3 (2000): 131-53.

McCracken, Ellen. *New Latina Narrative: The Feminine Space of Postmodern Ethnicity*. Tucson: University of Arizona Press, 1999.

Miller, Niel. "Argentina and Uruguay: Heartbreak Tango." Chapt. 7 of *Out in the World: Gay and Lesbian Life from Buenos Aires to Bangkok*. New York: Random House, 1992.

Montero, Oscar. "Before the Parade Passes By: Latino Queers and National Identity." *Radical America* 24.4 (1993): 15-26.

Muñoz, José Esteban. *Disidentifications: Queers of Color and the Performance of Politics*. Minneapolis: University of Minnesota Press, 1999.

Muñoz, Willy O. *Polifonía de la marginalidad: La narrativa de escritoras latinoamericanas*. Santiago: Editorial Cuarto Propio, 1999.

Patton, Cindy and Sanchez-Eppler, Benigno. *Queer Diasporas*. Durham: Duke University Press, 2000.

Prada, Ana Rebeca, Virginia Ayllón and Pilar Contreras, eds. *Encuentro: Diálogo sobre escritura y mujeres*. La Paz, Bolivia: Editorial Sierpe, 1999.

Pravisini-Gebert, Lizabeth and Margarita Fernández Olmos. *El placer de la palabra erótica femenina de América Latina*. México, D.F.: Editorial Planeta, 1991.

Preble-Niemi, Oralia, ed. *Afrodita en el trópico: Erotismo y construcción del sujeto femenino en obras de autoras centroamericanas*. Potomac: Scripta Humanistica, 1999.

Rodríguez, Elsa. *Sexualidad y cultura*. Santafé de Bogotá: Universidad Distrital Francisco José de Caldas, 1999.

Rodríguez Matos, Carlos. "Actos de Amor: Introducción al estudio de la poesía puertorriqueña homosexual y lesbiana." *Desde Este Lado/From This Side*. 1.2 (1990): 23-24.

Saldivar-Hull, Sonia. *Feminism on the Border: Chicana Gender Politics and Literature*. Berkeley: University of California Press, 2000.

Sandoval-Sánchez, Alberto and Nancy Saporta Sternbach, eds. *Puro Teatro: A Latina Anthology*. Tucson: University of Arizona Press, 2000.

Sarda, Alejandra. "Lesbians and the Gay Movement in Argentina." *NACLA Report on the Americas*. 31:4 (Jan-Feb, 1998): 40-41.

Schaefer-Rodríguez, Claudia. *Danger Zones: Homosexuality, National Identity, and Mexican Culture*. Tucson: University of Arizona Press, 1996

Shaw, Deborah. "Erotic or Political: Literary Representations of Mexican Lesbians." *Journal of Latin American Cultural Studies*. 5.1 (1996): 51-63.

Smith, Paul Julian. *The Body Hispanic, Gender and Sexuality in Spanish and Spanish American Literature*. Oxford: Oxford University Press, 1989.

_____. *Laws of desire: Questions of homosexuality in Spanish writing and film, 1960-1990*. Oxford, New York: Clarendon Press, Oxford University Press, 1992.

Svich, Caridad and María Teresa Marrero, eds. *Out of the Fringe: Contemporary Latina/Latino Theatre and Performance*. New York: Theatre Communications Group, 2000.

Vinuales, Olga. *Identidades lésbicas: discursos y prácticas*. Barcelona: Edicions Bellaterra, 2000.

Illustration by Jennifer Whiting

Tortilleras on the Prairie:
Latina Lesbians Writing the Midwest

Amelia María de la Luz Montes

SUMMARY. This article argues that there is a considerable, distinctive Latina lesbian cultural presence in the Midwest that cannot be sufficiently accounted for using prevalent East or West Coast models of Latina lesbian artistic representation. By examining the literary productions of Latina lesbians in and/or from the Great Plains, we can arrive at a new concept of the border and of what it means to be a Chicana or Latina lesbian. *[Article copies available for a fee from The Haworth Document Delivery Service: 1-800-HAWORTH. E-mail address: <docdelivery@haworthpress.com> Website: <http://www.HaworthPress.com> © 2003 by The Haworth Press, Inc. All rights reserved.]*

KEYWORDS. Latina lesbian literature, testimonios, Chicano studies, queer theory, Midwest, Great Plains

Author note: I am grateful to a number of colleagues and friends for the many discussions surrounding this topic and responses to earlier drafts of this essay: Norma Cantú, Barbara DiBernard, Rafael Grajeda, June Levine, Joy Ritchie, Sue Rosowski, Scott Walters, David Wishart, Madelyn Detloff, and Catriona Esquibel. Thank you Emily Levine, for your love of the Great Plains, and your tireless editorial work. This article is dedicated to all Latina lesbians on the Great Plains/Midwest borderlands.

[Haworth co-indexing entry note]: "Tortilleras on the Prairie: Latina Lesbians Writing the Midwest." Montes, Amelia María de la Luz. Co-published simultaneously in *Journal of Lesbian Studies* (Harrington Park Press, an imprint of The Haworth Press, Inc.) Vol. 7, No. 3, 2003, pp. 29-45; and: *Latina Lesbian Writers and Artists* (ed: María Dolores Costa) Harrington Park Press, an imprint of The Haworth Press, Inc., 2003, pp. 29-45. Single or multiple copies of this article are available for a fee from The Haworth Document Delivery Service [1-800-HAWORTH, 9:00 a.m. - 5:00 p.m. (EST). E-mail address: docdelivery@haworthpress.com].

Imagine a Latina lesbian narrative set in Nebraska.[1] The setting is the state capitol. It is a spring afternoon and the lilacs are blooming. A GLBT gathering is underway: over 400 people are holding hands, making a human chain around the capitol to support legislation against discrimination. There's a Chilean lesbian holding hands with her lover, a Mexican American lesbian couple waving to their friends, and a Chicana hugging her Jewish lover whose long black braid and dark skin could mark her for a Chicana as well. This narrative may not be what you might expect to find in Nebraska. Here are borderlands miles away from the southwest where most Latina *testimonios*, poetry, or fiction are written or recorded.[2] This article uncovers and critiques Latina lesbian writing that is emerging from a geographical area not commonly considered a place where Latina lesbians even exist: The Great Plains or The Midwest.[3] Their *testimonios,* poetry, and fiction reveal characteristics not particularly associated to established southwest writing. For example, instead of describing *la frontera* as "desert," they may describe *la frontera* as "prairie." This geographical difference is complex because it denotes a psychological, spiritual, cultural sensibility that does not fit into the stereotypical Latina/Chicana lesbian southwest. And because the Latina lesbian from the Midwest shapes a narrative from a midwestern perspective, she may be considered "less" Latina or Chicana or less "lesbian." Associating Latina lesbian writing solely with southwest Latina border experiences does not help southwest Latina lesbians either. It only ghettoizes their stories and prevents other voices from participating in what could be a rich palette of narratives. Therefore, in this volume of Latina lesbian arts, I refrain from attempting to establish a tradition of Latina lesbian writing. Instead, I argue for a reconsideration of border writing while also revisiting what it means to be a Chicana or U.S. Latina lesbian.

As early as 1987, Gloria Anzaldúa made sure to describe borderlands that stretched beyond the southwest. In her preface to *Borderlands/La Frontera: The New Mestiza,* she wrote:

> The psychological borderlands, the sexual borderlands and the spiritual borderlands are not particular to the Southwest. In fact, the Borderlands are physically present wherever two or more cultures edge each other, where people of different races occupy the same territory, where under, lower, middle and upper classes touch, where the space between two individuals shrinks with intimacy.

Indeed, Latina lesbian art needs to be inclusive of borderlands "not particular to the Southwest." Chicana writer Norma Cantú calls this "integrating geographical-specific sites as places for negotiating identity" (Cantú). Cantú has migrated up and down the Great Plains throughout her life. Her family network inhabits Laredo, Texas, in the south and Omaha, Nebraska, in the north. Cantú also received her doctorate from the University of Nebraska in Lincoln. She says the experience of living in Nebraska "broadened my world of Tejas into lands that were before and beyond the border. I could imagine my ancestors before the Spanish and Mexican influence, travelling north. It reconnected me to my indigenous self–not linked to Aztecs but the Great Plains tribes . . . you know, they [the Great Plains tribes] come down even now . . . [to] South Texas" (Cantú). Cantú, then, offers an alternative to the 1960s construction of "Aztlán," the imagined land of the Chicano heritage. Cantú's description of the Great Plains tribes connecting her to her indigenous self opens an expansive swath of geographic spaces where individuals for one reason or another find themselves and become influenced by where they live. Geographic spaces become sites for identity formation. The challenge is to have these voices available and in print so that multiple perspectives on Latina lesbian identity reach a wide audience of readers.

Today, when one looks at works which include Latina lesbian writing (anthologies either exclusively lesbian or not) such as *Compañeras: Latina Lesbians; Infinite Divisions; Chicana Lesbians: The Girls Our Mothers Warned Us About; This Bridge Called My Back; Making Face, Making Soul;* or *Telling to Live: Latina Feminist Testimonios*, the authors describe or write primarily from places other than the Midwest. The Southwest, California, or the East Coast is represented. It is true that a higher concentration of Latina and Chicana lesbian communities can be found on either coast. The Latina lesbian communities in the Midwest are clearly not as visible as, say, communities in San Francisco. This is not to say that these anthologies are not helpful to Latina lesbians living in the Midwest. In the preface to *Compañeras*, Juanita Ramos writes, "*Compañeras* allows Latina lesbians who live isolated from other lesbians to know that they are not alone" (xiii). Yet, for the midwestern Latina lesbian who is able to find out about such an anthology it would be heartening to read a story or poem with a midwest focus.[4] In her essay, "Lost in Space: Queer Geography and The Politics of Location," Sherri Inness writes that she is:

> concerned with the damaging effects of universalizing certain types of gay experiences while relegating others to a marginalized position. Studies of gay men and lesbians in San Francisco and New York are often universalized, whereas the work of those concentrating on other locations is particularized. Simply because the experiences of gay men and women in certain areas, such as San Francisco and New York are so visible, it is all too easy for writers, both academic and nonacademic, to assume that the experiences of such gays reflect the experiences of other gays in the rest of the United States. (136-137)

While Inness' argument focuses primarily upon queer geographic locations, it helps open the door toward more complex discussions of lesbian ethnic borders. The changing demographics of Latinas and Latinos in the United States underlines the need to rethink the way lesbian and gay experiences are being considered. In the last ten years, Latino population numbers have jumped in the states between New Jersey and Colorado. In Nebraska, for instance, Latinos are becoming a visible and viable presence. According to Professor Martin Ramírez, "They [Latinos] are from Guatemala, Mexico, El Salvador, California. . . . They populate every county in the state of Nebraska. Nebraska has Spanish language radio stations in Lincoln, Omaha, Grand Island, and Scottsbluff. One of Grand Island's state legislators is a Chicano: Ray Aguilar" (*La Vida*). Latinos are also in Kansas and Minnesota, many having arrived at the turn of the last century to work on the railroad or to farm. During the early part of the twentieth century, they came from Mexico; more recently, Chileans, Guatemalans, and Salvadorans have settled in the Midwest. Even in classic works of literature, Latinos figure in the Great Plains imagination. Jim Burden (a character in the novel, *My Ántonia*, by Nebraska writer Willa Cather) remembers learning about the Spanish explorer, Coronado, coming to the Midwest: "A farmer in the county north of ours, when he was breaking sod, had turned up a metal stirrup of fine workmanship, and a sword with a Spanish inscription on the blade . . . Father Kelly, the priest, had found the name of the Spanish maker on the sword, and an abbreviation that stood for the city of Cordova" (236).

Cather describes a Spanish colonizer on Midwest lands. The Mexicans and Latinos to arrive years later–mestizos–would be considered quite differently from Coronado.[5] Chicano scholar, Rafael Grajeda, in his article, "Chicanos: The Mestizo Heritage" writes:

> It is more than a curiosity of history that the two entrances into the Central Plains by the Spanish-speaking people were so strikingly dissimilar. . . . That the original explorers of the Central Plains were Spanish conquistadores, and the later immigrants were Mexican mestizos, is–in its irony–further instructive, for the very conditions of the poor in Mexico–those conditions which to a large degree "pushed" these people to the north–can be traced to the conquest and later colonization of that country by the very same conquistadores. (51)

To follow Grajeda's point, then, one can consider the Great Plains a historical site of mestizaje: the conquistadores who walked the Great Plains and colonized Mexico contributed to creating a mestizo class. These mestizo descendants continue to arrive on unfamiliar lands (as close to the border as El Paso,

Texas, and as north as Minneapolis, Minnesota), displaced from their familiar surroundings, looking to survive. This is the Chicana heritage–born of the oppressed and the oppressor–that Chicana and Latina lesbian writers such as Cherríe Moraga and Anzaldúa examine and reinterpret in their writings.[6] They describe the Chicana and Latina lesbian as twice oppressed: by the Anglo culture and by her own people because she chooses to love a woman. Anzaldúa foregrounds this theme when she writes of "The New Mestiza" in *La Frontera/Borderlands*. She describes a New Mestiza who is emerging from all borderlands which have disowned her:

> As a mestiza I have no country, my homeland cast me out; yet all countries are mine because I am every woman's sister or potential lover. (As a lesbian I have no race, my own people disclaim me; but I am all races because there is the queer of me in all races.) I am cultureless because, as a feminist, I challenge the collective cultural/religious male-derived beliefs of Indo-Hispanics and Anglos; yet I am cultured because I am participating in the creation of yet another culture, a new story to explain the world and our participation in it, a new value system with images and symbols that connect us to each other and to the planet. (102-103)

The Latina lesbian in the Midwest, therefore, is a "New Mestiza" who must negotiate a land whose dominant culture is not completely hers, a land whose politics is primarily homophobic and repressive, a land in which even her own family often does not wish to acknowledge her sexual orientation. It is within this landscape that the Midwest "New Mestiza" is emerging to tell her story.

* * *

With this in mind, I present the following *testimonios,* poetry, and fiction to reveal women who come from markedly different backgrounds and experiences and who have all been influenced or see their identity interwoven with what is considered the Midwest. In her longing for a land she once knew, the Latina lesbian may depict a mixture of homeland vs. new land environments: Galveston farmworker lands evoked upon a Chicago steel mill; the prairie seen through working class urban settings. These works reveal intersecting borders of the urban and rural, newly arrived and well established, Anglo traditions and Latina lesbian sensibilities. The Latina lesbian in the Midwest speaks of her complex heritage: Chicana and Apache, Mexican American, Chilean. The Latina writing from a Midwest perspective is, in many ways, free to experiment with identity since she is not within a large, visible community. And yet, because she lives in the Midwest (historically and politically, an Anglo-protestant con-

servative area of the United States) she must decide what traditions she will re-
tain and which she will discard, all the while creating new ones.

I focus first on *testimonios* because this genre has historical significance in
Latina literature. *Testimonio*, with its rich history, is important for the Latina
lesbian in the Midwest. It is a way for her to survive and acknowledge her presence in a world that often seeks to disregard or silence her. In the anthology
Telling to Live: Latina Feminist Testimonios, by the Latina Feminist Group,
the writers explain the importance of *testimonio* in feminist history:

> *Testimonio* has been critical in movements for liberation in Latin America,
> offering an artistic form and methodology to create politicized under-
> standings of identity and community. Similarly, many Latinas partici-
> pated in the important political praxis of feminist consciousness-raising.
> The "second wave" feminist movement honored women's stories and
> showed how personal experience contains larger political meaning.
> Other feminists have developed self-reflexive research methods and so-
> cial practices, creating oral histories and feminist ethnographies that cap-
> ture the everyday lives and stories of women. Drawing from these
> various experiences, *testimonio* can be a powerful method for feminist
> research praxis. (3)

Testimonio also figures as an important genre in Latina and Latino culture
since its emergence in the nineteenth century. American literature professor
Genaro Padilla, author of *My History, Not Yours: The Formation of Mexican
American Autobiography*, describes the impetus for the creation of *testimonio:*

> The rupture of everyday life experienced by some 75,000 people who in-
> habited the far northern provinces of Mexico in 1846 opened a terrain of
> discursive necessity in which fear and resentment found language in
> speeches and official documents that warned fellow citizens to accom-
> modate themselves to the new regime or at least to remain quiet lest they
> be hurt or killed outright; in personal correspondence in which anger and
> confusion were voiced to intimates; in poetry, *corridos* (ballads), and
> *chistes* (jokes) that made *los americanos* the subject of ironic humor, lin-
> guistic derogation, and social villainy; and in Spanish-language newspa-
> per editorials and essays that argued for justice and equality for Mexican
> Americans in the new regime. Autobiographical desire also arose as part
> of this discursive necessity: memory–shocked into reconstructing the
> past of another socionational life set squarely against experience in "an
> alien political system in an alien culture"–gave rise to an autobiographi-
> cal formation . . . (4)

Padilla describes a genre which arises out of oppressive circumstances, a literature of survival, of making meaning out of the injustice incurred upon a people whose land was invaded, whose livelihood in the homeland was threatened. Today, Latina lesbians, daughters of these cultural *antepasados*, continue to struggle, not only with a society that views them as "alien" in an Anglo world, but also within the Latino sphere. Carla Trujillo, editor and writer, explains that "[t]he issue of being a lesbian, a Chicana lesbian, is still uncomfortable for many heterosexual Chicanas and Chicanos, even (and especially) those in academic circles. Our culture seeks to diminish us by placing us in a context of an Anglo construction, a supposed *vendida* [traitor] to the race" (ix). Never did I personally feel this more palpably than when I taught a course I had designed at UC Santa Barbara (on the West Coast, no less) in 1999. I had titled the course "Latina Queer Cultural Production." I asked the students (many of whom were Latinos) to tell me why they had chosen to take this class. I was amazed to hear a good number of them tell me they were taking it because they never thought that a Latina could be lesbian. They believed only Anglos could be lesbians. This myth is pervasive within Latino communities. Trujillo's statement, written in 1991, is still true today, but by using what Padilla calls "discursive necessity," Latina lesbians seek to use *testimonio* to establish their presence, to express their "fear and resentment" at a world that, racially, is hostile to them, and to make sense of their own familial world, which oftentimes does not acknowledge or accept them. Within that familial world, the denial of a daughter's sexual orientation, coupled with internal racial struggles, makes it extremely difficult for a Latina lesbian to come to an understanding of herself. Yet, there are those who succeed despite what may seem insurmountable adversities. They, in turn, want to become visible to other Latina lesbians by sharing their perspectives. Often, *testimonio* is the preferred genre. The twenty-first century *testimonio* takes many forms, including phone transcriptions and e-mail transmittals.

In the following *testimonio,* originally sent by e-mail, Mechelle,[7] who identifies as a Mexican American lesbian, describes her experiences as a native of Kansas:

> Slowly I am developing an identity as a lesbian who is Mexican. Being third and fourth generation Kansan, my family purposely lost their identity for the purpose of being "American" and to "assimilate." My parents speak little Spanish. We did not speak it in the home. We are all named with anglo names. Our families wanted to blend as much as possible by adopting the values and standards of the dominant white culture. I learned early in my life to hate being Mexican. Being Mexican equated being lazy, dirty, unattractive, undesirable. As I matured and discovered my identity I

realized I wanted and needed to understand myself–my heritage–my own family. In the last few years I have spent time reading and studying about race, power, and privilege. Now I am forming a proud identity as a Mexican lesbian. . . . Learning about my culture is like healing a wound that has been open my entire life. People like me were not represented by the dominant society and media unless it was in a negative or subordinate position. I am in awe of the strength and resilience of Mexican women–my mother and grandmother being two representations. (Mechelle)

Mechelle's *testimonio* begins with the racial complexities of her heritage. In Mechelle's experience, her sexual orientation was not the primary struggle and yet, in her descriptions, creating a lesbian identity intersects with discovering her Mexican American identity. She had to go outside of the family circle to uncover both. She also had to come to terms with her family's internal racism and homophobia, which intersect and alternate at various moments within the family structure.

[A]ccepting and formulating my identity as a lesbian was a much easier process than being Mexican. It sounds strange I know, but being gay I could conceal and chose to come out when I wanted. Growing up, I was very aware that there were family members (first cousins) who were gay/lesbian. My family made comments and jokes about them but never treated them badly. I got the message that being homosexual was wrong but the family would not ostracize you if you chose to reveal yourself to others. . . . Living in a rural area, it was and still is difficult to meet other people like me. As a result, I had to formulate an identity based on the dominant stereotype of what a lesbian was supposed to be. To be exposed to the homosexual culture, I had to drive from Western Kansas to a city and that meant a three or four hour trip. Growing up I did not have music, magazines, books, and other cultural things readily available to me. . . . My family is very accepting of me as a daughter and sister. However, me being gay is not discussed. I am out to my brothers and sister-in-laws but not my sister. My parents know but I have not personally talked with them. They just know . . . especially my mom. I guess the silence is the lack of acknowledgement in the community (communities) where you are from–in my experience Latina women are at great risk if they do come out. It is a great risk to be a woman who does not "need a man." Therefore, invisibility is safe. [R]ural Kansas is very separated in terms of old Hispanic families and newer immigrant families. Older settled families are very prejudiced and discriminatory of the newer families settling in the area. (Mechelle)

* * *

Alejandra, a Chilean lesbian who has been living in Nebraska for ten years and sees the Midwest as her home now, has had markedly different experiences from Mechelle's.

> If you're a Mexican here, you almost have an automatic support network. But if you're not–like me from Chile–you're not part of the community. People assume that we're all the same. Maybe that's why the Latina and Hispanic name doesn't connect with me. I say I'm Chilean. I'm learning a lot about the Mexican community that's for sure. The Mexican community is a growing population here, so many feel they're taking over and so there's animosity here towards them. In Chile identity is different. No one over there says Latina or Hispanic. I never felt like I was discriminated over there. Everyone was Chilean. . . . I don't have many people here from my country. Even when people ask me about my country, I don't know anymore. What I know is from the past–and I don't even know how things have changed. I just know I couldn't be myself over there. That makes me more sad–because I couldn't have a job and be out or have a partner and be out about it. Society will reject me. Everything is taboo and underground. Everybody is afraid of coming out. . . . [T]his [Nebraska] is where I feel I'm more comfortable with myself and people are here who support me for who I am–my friends and other people who know I'm lesbian. I can be completely myself here. (Alejandra)

Alejandra's primary struggle in Chile, then, concerned her sexual orientation: "and that's why I live here," she says. "I think I'm an independent person and I feel like . . . like where I'm from as a woman you have less opportunities to grow personally and professionally. The machismo–you have less power over there." Here, Alejandra feels that there are different struggles. She believes it is important to have Chicana and Latina lesbian literature and art that represent the Midwest.

> I think it would be important because when you come out, you think you're the only one–especially in the Hispanic culture–we're less visible. I think it would help women to feel proud of their heritage and also to be lesbian. Lesbians and Hispanics are afraid to be out–and having someone renowned or known would create some pride. (Alejandra)

* * *

In poetry, Odilia Galván Rodríguez is one writer whose work represents the intersections of identity in a Midwest landscape. In examining one of her poems, I look at themes and motifs that have distinctly Midwestern origins. Rodríguez infuses a mestizaje (mix of cultures–Anzaldúa's *New Mestiza*) within the following poem that blends her Lipan, Apache, and Chicana heritage within a Great Plains (Galveston) and midwest (Chicago) landscape. Rodríguez was born in Galveston, Texas, and grew up within a farmworker family. She later moved to Chicago when her father took a job in the steel mills. Her poetry evokes the Mexican *corridos*, which are narrative poems focusing upon themes of displacement, nostalgia, and regeneration. In the poem "Ponies" she depicts the south Chicago Projects as "a prairie":

"Ponies"

My first pony blue
warrior made in the USA   1957
bought in 1987 for
one hundred dollars
a fortune to me then

Chevy with manual column shifting
no power steering   before stick
shifts were in   out again
back seat full of black top
        broken and spit
through a big hole in the floor

I grew up in a City of buses
the L snakes   winding
tunneling through the town
no reason to drive cars
Chicago Transit Authority
        for getting   around

Moms came from Texas
couldn't part with hers
so many old and broken down
kept them sitting in the railroad yard
behind the Projects where we lived

our prairie
though kids not allowed

because of hobos passing through
we'd disobey   make those cars forts
our motto   you can't hurt steel

holes in floors are nothing new
but a pony needs to be reliable
no matter what
even if people point
laugh at its looks

who cares   you know
theirs is probably no better
an old beater brought back to life
like those old mustangs waiting
in the junk yard   other '57's

those one-eyed fords of our youth
dappled with rust   painted primer gray
mufflers   held up
by duct tape and bailing wire
doors and trunks tied shut with climber's rope

Indian cars   part of our story
we're nations
proud of our ponies
these vehicles that give us hope[8]

The poem evokes a nostalgia, a loss of place, recounting a history while simultaneously creating new environments. "My first pony blue/warrior made in the USA   1957" locates the poem in time and country. The intersection of "pony" and "made in the USA" recounts colonization, industrial revolution, corporate economy, and a clash of cultures (Indian and White). Rodríguez distinguishes her "pony" as a "pony blue warrior," which connects to the Paint Horse of the Great Plains lore. The Paint Horse, which most often has blue eyes, has a rich history in the United States. Spanish explorers brought the horse to the prairies. According to the American Paint Horse Association (APHA), the horses the Spaniards brought to these lands included the Paint Horse–a spotted horse or what looks like a horse splashed with color (brown and white, or brown/black and white).[9] They are also associated with "the Mustang herds that spread across the Great Plains and gave the Indians a reservoir of breeding stock from which to draw. By the early 1800s, the West had thousands of wild horses. Prominent among these free-ranging herds . . . were Paints" (APHA). In the mid to late nineteenth century, however, the influx of Anglo-American culture and American industrialization replaced the horse with the railroad and later, the car. Rodríguez makes both the pony and the car her own. The "Chevy" becomes her free-ranging Paint horse but this one is of deteriorating metal. The car, ironically, becomes useful as building material for forts. Rodríguez is a transplant to Chicago where no cars are needed, where mass transit has become the necessary means of transportation. Chicago and the L, like "snakes winding/tunneling through the town . . ." is a line that contains an animal metaphor while the words "winding" and "tunneling" also bring to mind water, streams, or rivers that curve and bend through prairie landscapes. The mass transit of Chicago becomes for Rodríguez a remembrance of a rural world merged with steel and industry. Her Chevy and her mother's car that "came from Texas/couldn't part with hers" are "sitting in the railroad yard/behind the Projects where we lived/our prairie."

There is a sense of travel, of worlds and people migrating through histories and centuries. Rodríguez's writing describes what La Mestiza in the Midwest continues to do: she merges what often seems like disparate worlds in order to make meaning of them, in order to create new identities. Narrow definitions of the Latina lesbian do not apply here. Universalized notions of Latina or Chicana lesbian identity only lead to further stereotyping and marginalizations. Rodríguez presents a poem that particularizes one experience. In this poem, the world is broadened and reframed from Apache horses to "one-eyed fords of our youth/ dappled with rust   painted primer gray . . . Indian cars part of our story/we're nations/proud of our ponies" (Rodríguez 102). The poem's spaces around phrases like "our prairie" and "Indian cars" encourage a pause in order to invite the reader to consider connections between the urban and rural landscapes. These connections reveal Rodríguez's individual story–her own historical perspective–whose origin involves a history of painful and brutal assimilation. "[W]e're nations" reminds the reader that there are many tribes, many stories. Here is a poem that takes up the trope of nostalgia to depict a collage of memory, survival, and pride of heritage: "these vehicles that give us hope." Rodríguez creates a poem that integrates oppressive histories and personal memories with defiant pride.

* * *

Another writer, Adelita, a Latina lesbian living in Lawrence, Kansas, writes poetry and fiction with lesbian themes. Her latest work in progress is entitled, "Mujeres Tambien Lloran" ("Women Also Cry"). It is set in a *cantina* where women gather. Adelita describes the premise:

Fictional cantinas set in the midwest where we can cry as much as they [heterosexuals in Midwestern bars] can and we can sit in the *cantina* and talk about our lost loves. Generally, the story is about trying to have a normal life. The general theme is always having to hold back who you are. Here's the story. A character has just broken up with her partner. She starts listening to some old *boleros*. She's trying to feel that anguish drinking tequila in her kitchen and trying to re-create that atmosphere and she knows she's not in her atmosphere to do that. So she goes to one of the local gay bars and finds all these white boys listening to techno music. She can't find a way to feel her pain. (Adelita)

What the main character needs is the familiar sound of the *bolero* in a *cantina* setting in order to grieve the loss of her lover. The story of community and safe places to share one's pain is not unfamiliar and could be a story set in Los Angeles or New York. But this is the Midwest. Although local gay bars do exist here, specifically Latina lesbian *cantinas* may be scarce (even in cosmopolitan cities), but the author works to create such a place on the Great Plains. To avoid stereotypes, Adelita's gay bar does not play western or country music. It is playing "techno"–a sound expected in cosmopolitan cities like San Francisco. Adelita creates a story that has unexpected ingredients: *boleros* and tequila, a Latina lesbian *cantina*, women, and community.

I tend to be misunderstood by some other lesbians because they say why am I focusing so much on the Latina culture. I should be focusing on being a lesbian. For example, I hate folk music. I don't like the Indigo Girls. I want to hear *Rancheras*. And so some of my friends kid me and say that I'm not a real lesbian. I think that I have other battles to fight than some of my other lesbian sisters. Two major battles are, being Latina and being the lesbian. I feel I have to choose one or the other. I do get criticism that I am a Latina who happens to be a lesbian instead of a lesbian who is Latina. (Adelita)

Adelita grew up in a rural town north of Dallas, Texas. She says, "I did not meet a Latina lesbian until I got here in the Midwest. I came to Iowa and met my first Latina lesbian and she was from Argentina and then I met another one. [H]ere (in Lawrence, Kansas) there are a number of Latina lesbians" (Adelita). Adelita enjoys where she now lives, is part of a small lesbian community, and does not see herself moving back to Texas. However, living in the Midwest still means being less visible than if she were in Los Angeles or New York. "For one, I think because of the nature of where we're living, we're taught to be more low key about who we are. . . . [T]he Midwest has the 'traditional family values.' They won't accept you because you're brown, and so for those of us in the Midwest, we have to be very careful and not be out as much." Adelita wishes Latina lesbians from more visible areas of the country would connect with her and other Latina lesbian communities in the Midwest:

> I really wish that sometimes our Latina lesbian sisters on the east or west coast could give us a shout out and acknowledge the fact that we have to keep quiet about our lifestyle. Because of the fact that we don't have all of the access to our culture–there aren't radio stations playing the latest music, we don't know who the artists are that are cool right now. We don't have celebrations for Cinco de Mayo. We don't have the rituals here that make them think we're Latinas. But they fail to notice that we have the brown skin that makes us Latina because we still have to deal with the racism. (Adelita)

* * *

What happens, then, when a Latina does have the connections to the East or West Coast? I conclude with one more *testimonio* that particularizes the experience of being from the West Coast and assimilating to the Midwest. Claudia is a Kansas resident who was born in Los Angeles, California, and lived there for eight years before moving to the Midwest (southwest Missouri and then Kansas). She still has family in Los Angeles whom she visits, but feels strongly about being a Midwesterner. "I have become accustomed to the culture of the Midwest and my family in Los Angeles even says I am a Midwesterner." It was in the Midwest that Claudia realized she was lesbian.

> I think my culture has carried some traditions into the way I am a lesbian. I find myself trying to be somewhat traditional in my relationship with my partner. Family is still equally important to me as a lesbian and I think that stems from the Latino culture. Basically, my Latina culture has made me the type of lesbian I am. . . . My lesbian identity has always come second. I struggle enough in the Midwest by trying to be Latina that being lesbian gets bumped to second place. Being Latina is much more obvious, in terms of appearance, than being lesbian. I am just starting to grow more as a lesbian, and I have much to learn. More specifically, I find it interesting to find other lesbian Latinas. Not so much as interesting, maybe more of a miracle for the Midwest. [I]t is important for more Latina lesbians to be represented in all regions of the U.S. . . . Yes, Latina lesbians do exist! (Claudia)

Through *testimonio,* poetry, and fiction, Latina lesbians who are writing and speaking from a Midwestern experience are loudly voicing the varied and rich Latina lesbian identities within the United States at this time. Even if I were focusing upon the more well-known California Latina lesbian writers and artists, there would still be a difference of perspectives: East L.A. and Santa Monica or the San Francisco Mission district and Berkeley. "Only by recognizing that place is as crucial an element in shaping queer identities as is history can lesbians and gay men hope to create a queer studies that more fully understands the various perspectives of the people for whom it claims to speak," writes Sherry Inness (156). For me, collecting *testimonios* and reading poetry by Latina lesbians in this Midwestern landscape that is still so new to me have forced me to theorize what it means for me, a Chicana lesbian from Los Angeles, to be living in Nebraska. My preconceived notions of the Midwest and my own adherence to an "authentic" Chicana identity were, thankfully, erased–but not without much critical and personal exploration.

Landlocked Nebraska, far from West Coast horizons and southern borders, is shaping the way I daily place myself in it. As I continue to write from this landscape, my writing will be different from what it was in Los Angeles, reflecting not only ocean waters, but prairie fields. The beginning of this article, for example, took us to the steps of the Nebraska state capitol where Latina lesbians joined other lesbians, gays, transgendered, transsexuals, allies, in one voice last April–to demand protections not now afforded us in this state. We held hands, making a human chain around the capitol. The faces and voices we saw and heard were not exactly the lesbians we see in the media or in the photos of lesbian protest rallies published in academic queer theory texts. Our skin may be various shades of brown, our hair long rather than short, and our earrings may jingle–something one might expect in Los Angeles from straight Latinas, though even that can be a false image. But we're here in the Midwest–destabilizing what it means to be Chicana and lesbian, reconsidering what it means to have a tradition of Latina lesbian arts. It is extremely important not to universalize and position an already overly marginalized community in a fixed framework of construction. The New Mestiza lives in large cosmopolitan communities as well as in small rural towns in underpopulated states, and we need to give voice to them and every Mestiza in between. This is an invitation to rethink queer theoretical positions of identity and cultural production–an invitation to imagine a multitudinous nation and world of varying experiences and perspectives.

NOTES

1. Throughout this article, the following terms will be used: Latina, Chicana, Mexican American. Because this volume uses the term "Latina," I will more often use that term which denotes women who are either Latin American women or descendants of Latin American parents born and/or living in the United States. Not all women who have connections to these areas will choose to call themselves Latina. Some choose to call themselves Chicana which originates from the sixteenth-century name, "Mexicana." "Mexicana" derives from the Nahuatl "Mexica," meaning a people who live in the center of the maguey (cactus plant). "Mexicana" in sixteenth-century speech was articulated as "Meshicana" and later altered in the twentieth century to Chicana. In the 1960s, Mexican Americans living in the southwest and especially in the southern California area adopted the name Chicana in order to privilege their indigenous inheritance. Chicana is a political term, a term denoting one who is politically active for the rights of Mexican Americans/Latinas. Some women choose the term Mexican American, which defines, specifically, that they are descendants of Mexican parents born and/or living in the United States. I choose not to use the term Hispanic. Hispanic continues to be a controversial term. In the 1980s, the Reagan administration instituted a Hispanic Month which automatically placed all Latinas (Mexican Americans, Puerto-Rican Americans, Cuban-Americans, etc.) within a peninsular Spanish historical context. The government also designed census forms and other legal documentation to denote all Latinas as Hispanic. Some groups do claim true lineage from Spain or Hispania. For example, various communities in New Mexico (Taos, Santa Fe) claim Hispanic identity. However, it is important to note that Latinas should not be considered Hispanic collectively.

2. *Testimonio* literally means to give witness, to declare. *Testimonios* can be written or oral.

3. The Great Plains and the Midwest are terms that are often written about in the same context as if they were one region. And to some geographers, historians, and literary scholars, the Great Plains and the Midwest are interchangeable terms. For the sake of this article, however, it is important to explain why and how these terms are used. The Great Plains has been defined as the area stretching from Manitoba in the north to Texas in the south and from the Missouri River in the east to the Rocky Mountains in the west. According to geographer, David Wishart, in Lincoln, Nebraska we are in an area called "the western extension of the Midwest or the eastern extension of the Great Plains. The more accurate description is the Midwest." For this article, I choose to use both terms in order to resist any fixed description of this area.

4. Currently this particular anthology–*Compañeras: Latina Lesbians*–is out of print.

5. Mestizos are mixed-blood people whose descendants are both indigenous and of European descent (primarily Spanish).

6. More than once I have quoted Cherríe Moraga when I write of the intersections of the oppressed/oppressor within the Chicana/Latina heritage. Moraga clearly describes and takes ownership of a heritage that is both "indigena" and "conquistador"–the colonized and the colonizer. In *The Last Generation*, she writes, "Most Mexicans can claim the same but my claim is more 'explorer' than not. . . . We must open the wound to heal, purify ourselves with the prick of Maguey thorns" (122 & 192). Moraga (who is herself born of bicultural parents–Anglo and Mexican) seeks to uncover these two divergent points of identity in order to create, much like Anzaldúa describes, a new identity. Anzaldúa calls this The New Mestiza. Moraga sees this as a spiritual healing and strengthening of the Chicana identity.

7. Most of the Latina lesbians who participated in sharing their *testimonios* chose a pseudonym.

8. This poem was originally published in *Sinister Wisdom: A Journal for the Lesbian Imagination in the Arts and Politics*. Thus, this poem is situated within the realm of Chicana lesbian narrative, although the poet herself does not identify as lesbian. In addition to *Sinister Wisdom*, her work has also appeared in numerous women's, feminist, people of color, lesbian and political journals, magazines and anthologies such as *Matrix Women's News Magazine, Color Life, Redwood Cultural Work* and others.

9. According to historians James C. Olson and Ronald C. Naugle:

> When first acquired from the Southwest in the early eighteenth century, the horse greatly modified life for the plains Indians. Traditional aspects of plains culture such as the tipi, the travois for transportation, the controlled buffalo hunt, and many ceremonies were reorganized around the horse. It allowed a greater emphasis on hunting and less on horticulture, and tribes such as the Cheyennes abandoned the permanent village for the nomadic camp. Others, like the Pawnees, retained their permanent villages but intensified their hunting activities. (26)

BIBLIOGRAPHY

Adelita. *testimonio* interview, 17 August 2002.

Alejandra. *testimonio* interview, 3 July 2002.

American Paint Horse Association. "History of the Paint Horse," online article, 1 Feb. 1995. *Horse Previews Magazine* <www.horse-previews.com>.

Anzaldúa, Gloria. *Borderlands/La Frontera: The New Mestiza.* 2ⁿᵈ ed. San Francisco: Aunt Lute Books, 1999.

Anzaldúa, Gloria, ed. *Making Face, Making Soul/Haciendo Caras: Creative and Critical Perspectives by Feminists of Color.* San Francisco: Aunt Lute Books, 1990.

Cantu, Norma. e-mail interview, 4 July 2002.

Cather, Willa. *My Ántonia.* 1918. Ed. Charles Mignon. Lincoln: University of Nebraska Press, 1994.

Claudia. *testimonio* interview, 27 June 2002.

Grajeda, Rafael. "Chicanos: The Mestizo Heritage." *Broken Hoops and Plains People.* Nebraska: Nebraska Curriculum Development Center, 1976.

La Vida: A Journey of Latinos Throughout Nebraska. Dir. Jayne SebbyProd. Nebraska ETV Network (NETCHE), Inc. Dist. Great Plains National, 2001.

Mechelle. *testimonio* interview, 3 July 2002.

Moraga, Cherríe. *The Last Generation: Prose and Poetry.* Boston: South End Press, 1993.

Moraga, Cherríe and Gloria Anzaldúa, eds. *This Bridge Called My Back: Writings by Radical Women of Color.* New York: Kitchen Table, 1983.

Olson, James C. and Ronald C. Naugle. *History of Nebraska.* 3rd ed. Lincoln: University of Nebraska Press, 1997.

Padilla, Genaro M. *My History Not Yours: The Formation of Mexican American Autobiography.* Wisconsin: The University of Wisconsin Press, 1993.

Ramos, Juanita, ed. *Compañeras: Latina Lesbians: An Anthology.* New York: Routledge, 1994.

Rebolledo, Tey Diana and Eliana S. Rivero, eds. *Infinite Divisions: An Anthology of Chicana Literature.* Tucson: University of Arizona Press, 1993.

Rodríguez, Odilia Galván. "Ponies." *Sinister Wisdom: A Journal for the Lesbian Imagination in the Arts and Politics.* 58 (1998): 101-102.

The Latina Feminist Group. *Telling to Live: Latina Feminist Testimonios.* Durham: Duke University Press, 2001.

Trujillo, Carla, ed. *Chicana Lesbians: The Girls Our Mothers Warned Us About.* Berkeley: Third Woman Press, 1991.

Wishart, David. personal interview. 12 June 2002.

The Role of Carmelita Tropicana in the Performance Art of Alina Troyano

Tonya López-Craig

SUMMARY. This article maps out the development and cultural meanings in the performance art of Alina Troyano, better known by her stage name, Carmelita Tropicana. Through such strategies as code switching, the avoidance of commodification, the development of alter egos, the breaking of heterosexist norms, and the creation of an intercultural discourse, Troyano has created a hybrid identity as an artist and performer. *[Article copies available for a fee from The Haworth Document Delivery Service: 1-800-HAWORTH. E-mail address: <docdelivery@haworthpress.com> Website: <http://www.HaworthPress. com> © 2003 by The Haworth Press, Inc. All rights reserved.]*

KEYWORDS. Carmelita Tropicana (Alina Troyano), performance art

Hello people, you know me, I know you. I am Carmelita Tropicana. I say Loisada is the place to be. It is multicultural, multinational, mucho multi. And like myself, you've got to be multilingual. I am very good with the tongue. As a matter of fact the first language I pick up when I come to

---

Tonya López-Craig is a photographer and artist. She has had several shows in the Los Angeles area.

[Haworth co-indexing entry note]: "The Role of Carmelita Tropicana in the Performance Art of Alina Troyano." López-Craig, Tonya. Co-published simultaneously in *Journal of Lesbian Studies* (Harrington Park Press, an imprint of The Haworth Press, Inc.) Vol. 7, No. 3, 2003, pp. 47-56; and: *Latina Lesbian Writers and Artists* (ed: María Dolores Costa) Harrington Park Press, an imprint of The Haworth Press, Inc., 2003, pp. 47-56. Single or multiple copies of this article are available for a fee from The Haworth Document Delivery Service [1-800-HAWORTH, 9:00 a.m. - 5:00 p.m. (EST). E-mail address: docdelivery@haworthpress.com].

47

New York is Jewish. I learn from my girlfriend Charo, she's Jewish. She teach me and I write poem for her in Jewish. I recite for you today. Title of the poem is "Oy Vey Number One." "Oy Vey, I schlep and schlep, I hurt my tuchus today, I feel–meshunggener, oy vey." (Applause) Danke, danke, danke. (Troyano 137)

During the early 1960s seven-year-old Alina Troyano moved from her native Cuba to the United States. Her father, whom Troyano has called a revolutionary, fled with his family after Fidel Castro's revolution overthrew dictator Fulgencio Batista. Of Troyano's exile Chon Noriega says the following: "In short, she is a member of what Gustavo Peréz Firmat calls the '1.5 generation.' It is a generation whose 'exile' is lived through their parents' memories and modified by American mass culture" (X). This crucial change in Troyano's young life would later appear throughout her work and specifically in *Memorias de la Revolución/Memories of the Revolution* and *Milk of Amnesia*.

In 1983 Alina Troyano began her stage career with stand-up comedy at the 11th Street WOW cafe in New York City that would later aid her in her signature method of social commentary through humor. Art, at this time, reflected social changes, such as the presidential election of Ronald Reagan, the anti-feminist counterattacks by conservative groups (or, as it was often termed, "postfeminism") and a move in the art market toward an endorsement of "neo-expressionism, a macho reaction to the pluralism generated by '70s feminism, which had threatened the white male stronghold in the visual arts" (Hammond 51). While there was a surge of production from gay and lesbian artists and artists of color in the 1970s that did indeed append the postmodern discourse of pluralism, prospects were few for those outside of the mainstream heterosexist and racially prejudiced world of art.

In her book *I, Carmelita Tropicana: Performing Between Cultures*, Troyano addresses the conditions in which she was creating art during this time:

> Art was more about process than product, more about esthetic edification than career, more about transgression than mainstream assimilation. It was the worst of times: AIDS hit, clubs and galleries closed, the NEA started defunding, the culture wars began. But back to the happy times when my life changed. (XIV)

This life change transpired when she discovered that she could reject the margins inside which she had been placed by the central authority of the dominant culture and express her unique voice through performance: "It is precisely this aspect of performance art–the opportunity it makes available to 'women of color' to use their racialized and sexualized bodies as a metaphor to disrupt and challenge the dominant system of representation–that makes this medium so attractive to Latinas and others" (Arrizón 136). Performance art, born out from the work of 1950s avant-garde artists and the happenings of the 1960s, had a strong influence on artists working outside the mainstream. This medium that abandoned the sacred "art object" and often utilized the voice and body bestowed an occasion to assert, be seen, and request that the audience take notice of the marginalized artist. Coco Fusco discusses performance artists' use of the various venues: Some of those histories that focus on the social significance of the dematerialization of the object also stress that performance artists displaced the collector as ideal consumer, favoring instead an audience of peers, and sought to take their work outside the mechanisms of the commodification by situating it in noninstitutional, and later in artist-run nonprofit spaces (8).

The WOW cafe group was one of such places. It was, according to Troyano, "a place where the credo for every women was 'Express Yourself.' A place that said if existing theatre does not represent women like us, let us create that theatre " (Troyano XIV). WOW was an enclave where a mostly lesbian crowd, could come and exhibit their art, read poetry, and go to workshops "in butch femme, and stand-up comedy" (Troyano XIV). In Alina Troyano's first performances at WOW she was cast for three characters in Holly Hughes' *The Well of Horniness*, Al Dente, Chief of Police, and Georgette, whom Troyano described as a "butch girl":

> Playing butch hit closer to home. All those voices from my adolescence came back to haunt me: "Don't laugh that loud." "Don't walk that way, pareces una carretonera." "You look like a truck driver." I had been sent to charm and etiquette school to cure my gruff demeanor. Now I was being asked to play a butch girl and revel in it. When I stepped on stage, took off my shirt exposing bare arms in a tank T-shirt, and flexed my muscles, the girls went "Oooh." I had a revelation: This wasn't so bad. (XIV)

It was during this time that Alina developed her alter ego Carmelita Tropicana. Through this comical personality, Troyano could relate her unique worldview without feeling overly exposed during her early stand-up routines. At WOW she studied with a teacher whose advice centered on mainstream acceptance by entering the club circuit as well as television shows like David Letterman's. Troyano explains her reaction to her teacher's advice:

> She warned me about using foreign words and expressions that middle America, the target audience, was not familiar with. Chutzpah and oy vey had to go. But the sensuous pleasure I got from rolling meshuggener around my lips and tongue I couldn't give up, or the idea of teaching a vocabulary word or playing in the backyard of a different culture. (Troyano XV)

This was the critical push that the self-proclaimed "Carmelita Tropicana, Ms. Lower East Side Beauty Queen, Famous Night Club, Superintendent, Performance Artiste" needed to decide seeking her own route and following her own objectives. Her character Carmelita Tropicana, referred to as a "bold synthesis of cubanidad (Cuban-ness), lesbian sexuality, and female spectacle" (X), could now be developed into a critical force for deconstruction of Latina, lesbian, and female stereotypes.

Through her performance art and, more specifically, through her character Carmelita Tropicana, Troyano confronts myths about the Latina and the lesbian, by assuming the extreme stereotypes that both social groups hold and performing them through her unique brand of humor. While undertaking the role of Latina lesbian, she also incorporates diverse characteristics distinct to other racial, ethnic, and national groups. The result is not only a debunking of the essentialist myth of what "Latinidad" is, but also a creation of hybrids that simultaneously produce de-mythicization of the racial, ethnic and/or national markers, and close in on what Carmelita Tropicana represents: a recognition and appreciation of the "other": In Chon Noriega's view, Troyano uses her autobiographical voice to "make an appeal on the basis of a unity rooted in colonialism–which is to say, othering–rather than humanism" (XII).

Her repetition of the prefix multi ("multi, multi, multi"), quoted in the beginning of this essay, fundamentally encompasses the essence of Troyano's work. Noriega goes on to explain: "Troyano's works place race and ethnicity into play with gender and sexuality. But rather than define a uniquely composite identity (that is, base her authority on being a Cuban lesbian artist), Troyano prefers to be 'very good with the tongue,' using language to conjure up the multiple characters and social relations that define America at the end of the millennium" (XII). Throughout her performance piece/play *Chica 2000* Troyano uses code switching. Tropicana's character and her two clones repeatedly speak in the following terms:

> Clana–"Where are you from, girl?"
> Cluna–"The Bronx, France. Je parle Français. And you?"
> Clana–"Miami, Cuba. Mucho Spanglish."
> [. . .]
> Cluna–"Relax sister. You're safe with me. Moi et vous, in this cave, c'est toute."
> Clana–"I feel very connected, like we had to meet."
>
> Cluna–"We're two peas in a pod."
> Clana–"Corta' por la misma tijera." (103)

In the course of the amalgamation of languages throughout her work, she demonstrates a resistance to the myth of an English-only, homogenized America. Descriptions, such as that of her cherished Lower East Side in New York ("Loisada") as "multicultural, multinational, mucho multi" and "multilingual," are representative of Troyano's rejection of boundaries in her work.

Likewise, she consistently employs sexual innuendo and sexuality itself to foster a breakage of the heterosexist boundaries dominant society places on Latinas, lesbians, and women in general. Troyano also confronts the stereotype of the macho Latino man through her character Pingalito Betancourt, whom Troyano plays in *Memorias de la Revolución, Milk of Amnesia* and *Chicas 2000*. Among the many topics expounded by Betancourt, one of them is Puritanism in *Chicas 2000*:

> But where I part company with Puritanism is with the sexuality stuff. I think there is a little hypocrisy here. How many of you remember Jocelyn Elders? Come on, raise your hands. For those of you who don't know, Jocelyn Elders was the surgeon general who dared to mention masturbation. And what happened to her? She got fired. I want to take a poll today. Raise your hands ladies and gentlemen if you have never ever touched yourselves. Come on. OK.
>
> So, people, Puritanism has some good things some bad. How do we save it? We cannot throw the baby out with the bathwater. How do we create a gentler, kinder Puritanism? (73-74)

Bedecked with a guayabera and a cigar, Pingalito Betancourt is the manifested Latino stereotype that is often present in many characteristics of Carmelita Tropicana. Through Tropicana and Betancourt, Troyano speaks candidly about sex and confronts narrow-minded heterosexist fears of sexual encounters outside what is naively deemed "the norm." Troyano uses Pingalito Betancourt in her performance to critique the idea of an essential feminine mystique and adoration of this mythical ideal by men as well as to further explicate the objectification of women.

In both *Milk of Amnesia* and *Memorias de la Revolución* Pingalito delivers a speech about his native homeland Cuba:

> This is the most beautiful land that human eyes have seen. The majestic mountains of La Sierra Maestra. Our mountains, not too tall. We don't need high. If we get snow, then we gotta buy winter coat. And the beaches of Varadero! But, ladies and gentlemen, none can compare with the beauty of the human landscape. Óyeme, mano. Estas coristas de Tropicana. With the big breast, thick legs. In Cuba we call girls carros,

and I mean your big American cars. Your Cadillac, no Toyota or Honda. Like the dancer Tongolele. I swear to you people, or my name isn't Pingalito Betancourt, you could put a tray of daiquiris on Tongolele's behind, and she could walk across the floor without spilling a single drop. That, ladies and gentlemen is landscape. For that you give me a gun and I fight for that landscape. Not oil. You gotta have priorities. (Troyano 54, Sandoval-Sanchez 398)

Through this character there is, as Jesús Hernandez states, "a complication of identity and identifiers" (*Alina Troyano in Cuban America*). Hernández elaborates on the implications of the character: "By completely achieving the enactment of the Cuban American male stereotype, Troyano, as a queer woman defies the very constructions of this stereotype; if Troyano, as a queer woman can convincingly perform the stereotype of the Cuban American straight man, then any possible chance of validity for this image is shattered" (*Alina Troyano in Cuban America*). By appropriating and aligning disparate characters, such as those of Betancourt and Tropicana, Troyano achieves the dissolution of boundaries placed by societal stereotypes of Latinas, lesbians, Cubans and women.

In *Milk of Amnesia* Troyano addresses her own distinct experience of exile from Cuba and delves into issues of personal identity and memory. In an interview with Ana López and Daniel Balderston after a performance at Tulane University, Troyano explained the following: "*Milk of Amnesia* tries to work with what I am right now, trying to figure that out, and to work out how Carmelita and I–Alina, the writer–are split. So it's like trying to play with the realities that I found in Cuba, trying to go back and see something" (*Memories and More Memories*). In *Milk of Amnesia,* Troyano's Carmelita Tropicana revisits Cuba in order to uncover lost memories of a space that is internal to both the character and the author. In fact, Troyano's actual trip to Cuba in 1993 inspired her to write *Milk of Amnesia.*

In a 1995 interview with David Roman, Alina Troyano encapsulated her doubts about her Cuban identity asking, "If I went back [to Cuba], would the Cubans living in Cuba think that I wasn't Cuban? Would I have an accent? Would I be too American? All these things actually happened when I went to Cuba. At first, they would wonder: But who are you? I spoke Spanish, but other factors of my identity didn't register as Cuban for them–my gold knapsack, my high-top sneakers, my leopard Day-Glo shorts! They were confused about my identity."

(*Alina Troyano in Cuban America*)

In the course of the performance of *Milk of Amnesia* the audience is presented with thoughts on Cuban exile and identity by narrative voices of both Carmelita Tropicana and the author herself. In *Milk of Amnesia* we have a partial view of what life was like for the young Troyano during the years she was struggling with the daunting task of trying to integrate into the mainstream culture of the United States:

> Carmelita–In the morning I went to school. Our Lady Queen of martyrs. That's when it happened. In the lunchroom. I never drank my milk. I always threw it out. Except this time when I went to throw it out, the container fell and spilled on the floor. The nun came over. Looked at me and the milk. Her beady eyes screamed: You didn't drink your milk, Grade A pasteurized, homogenized, you Cuban refugee.
>
> After that day I changed. I knew from my science class that all senses acted together. If I took off my glasses, I couldn't hear as well. Same thing happened with my taste buds. If I closed my eyes and held my breath I could suppress a lot of flavor I didn't like. This is how I learned to drink milk. It was my resolve to embrace America as I chewed on my peanut butter and jelly sandwich and gulped down my milk. The new milk had replaced the sweet condensed milk of my Cuba. My amnesia had begun. (53)

The distress produced by the tension between the exile's need to hold on to her culture and the new society's demand for assimilation is apparent throughout this performance. In addition to the grief of being displaced from her homeland, Carmelita/Troyano suffered the added dimension of the exile-like condition imposed by the normative heterosexual society to a lesbian: "To the extent that lesbians can be spoken of as 'a people' at all, to the extent that there are such things as lesbian identities, these identities are injured by heterosexist oppression. Lesbians have faced continuous deprivation of social resources that we need; denied membership as lesbians in our societies, we find ourselves forced to speak in language of heterosexual, male-dominated regimes" (Phelan 119).

Troyano's choice to perform and convey both the physical and inner exile serves to propel the audience into the space occupied by Carmelita Tropicana. The audience is simultaneously confounded by Troyano's use of flashbacks, nonchronological time, and unusual stage elements in *Milk of Amnesia* and drawn in by her vulnerability, codified by her use of autobiographical accounts, humor, and the sharing of private reflections on her experience:

Carmelita– [. . .] I remember. We are all connected, not through AT&T, e-mail, Internet, but through memory, history, herstory, horsetory. I remember. (*She shadow boxes as she recites the poem.*)
I remember
Que soy de allí
Que soy de aquí
Un pie en New York (a foot in New York)
Un pie en La Habana (a foot in Havana)
And when I put a foot in Berlin (cuando pongo pata en Berlin)
I am called
A lesbische cubanerin
A woman of color
Culturally fragmented
Sexually intersected
But I don't split
I am fluid and interconnected
Like tie-dye colors I bleed
A Cuban blue sky an American pumpkin orange
Que soy de allá
Que soy de aquí (69-70)

Troyano regularly employs interculturalism to speak for and to those feeling the confines of the dominant mainstream existence. While she uses her work to convey the experience of Latina and lesbian women, successfully expanding the discourse of both, she also seeks to connect with the reality of difference that exists within these identities. Her body of work rejects a singular concept of a Latina, lesbian, or Latina lesbian and speaks against essentialist ideas: "Thus interculturalism as it is negotiated in Tropicana's performing identity regulates the claims of diverse orders of being, various sexualities, historicities, etc." (Arrizón 151). By creating hybrid identities, she welcomes everyone to play a part, at the same time that she transmits her longing for social and political change.

These hybrid identities encapsulate the views of Troyano's own existence that she herself cannot contain into one all-encompassing appellation. She presents a way of understanding otherness by showing that ultimately everyone is "the other" to someone. Her work calls into question the dominant demand that seeks to place individuals into tidy categories, and to label who and what they are, thus replacing the individual experience with the experience that is deemed standard by the majority. Troyano's productions expose the need to consider understanding beyond hegemonic conceptions. Troyano's refusal to align herself to a unified lesbian experience responds to her need to express her unique experience as a Latina and to embrace her cultural influences from Cuba, New York, the art world, and her economic conditions: "The effort to construct a singular 'woman' will inevitably leave out the lives of those who do not have the hegemonic power of description. This translates not only into bad theory but into bad politics, as white middle-class women set the legal and political agenda for women" (Phelan 5).

Alina Troyano locates herself with her character Carmelita Tropicana in a specific community of lesbian artists, like that from the WOW cafe. While she assists in increasing a lesbian artistic presence in this community she also contributes to the understanding and awareness that the lesbian community is further empowered by their exploration of difference.

Troyano's use of the prefix "multi" symbolizes the relevance of "difference" and plurality in her work. Her emphasis on the difference and the multiple realities relays an aspiration to engage as many people as she can, while still maintaining her own unique voice. Through her art, Alina Troyano exposes her repudiation of boundaries and invites the viewers to follow her example. Troyano believes in the uniqueness of every human being and recognizes the need to value and respect the differences they hold.

> Carmelita– [. . .] I agree with Pedro Luis and I want to leave you with a song by him called 'Todos por lo Mismo,' a song that says it best:
> Everybody for the same thing
> Between the pages of colonialism
> Capitalists, homosexuals, atheists, spiritualists, moralists
> Everybody for the same thing (Troyano 71)

WORKS CITED

Arrizón, Alicia. *Latina Performance. Traversing the Stage.* Bloomington: Indiana University Press, 1999.

Fusco, Coco. "Latin American Performance and the Reconquista of Civil Space." *Corpus Delecti. Performing Art of the Americas.* Ed. Coco Fusco. London: Routledge, 2000. 1-20.

Hammond, Harmony. *Lesbian Art in America.* New York: Rizzoli International Publications, Inc., 2000.

Hernández, Jesús. "Alina Troyano in Cuban America: Hybridity in the Performance Between Cultures." *Cuban/American Media Page.* 20 Dec. 2001 <www.brown.edu/Courses/EL0176/hybridity.htm> 1 Nov. 2002.

"Memories and More Memories: A Conversation with Carmelita Tropicana (Alina Troyano)," *South: Cultural Studies in the Americas.* Eds. López, Ana M., and Daniel Balderston. 1994. The Roger Thayer Stone Center for Latin American Studies,

Tulane University <www.tulane.edu/~spanport/SOUTH/I/interview.html> Nov. 1, 2002.

Phelan, Shane. *Getting Specific. Postmodern Lesbian Politics*. Minneapolis: University of Minnesota Press, 1994.

Troyano, Alina. *I, Carmelita Tropicana. Performing Between Cultures*. Boston: Beacon Press, 2000.

Troyano, Alina and Uzi Parnes. "Memorias de la Revolución." *Puro Teatro, A Latina Anthology*. Eds. Alberto Sandoval-Sánchez and Nancy Saporta Sternbach. Tucson: The University of Arizona Press, 2000. 391-424.

Moving *La Frontera*
Towards a Genuine Radical Democracy
in Gloria Anzaldúa's Work

Alejandro Solomianski

SUMMARY. This article situates Gloria Anzaldúa's work *Borderlands/La Frontera* in the context of staid, heterosexist academia and conventional readings of the Latin American mestizaje to show how the book has subverted both. By examining how *Borderlands* has been received and how it ironically anticipates these hierarchical readings, we can see the functioning of the elitist, exclusionary processes that manufacture subaltern identities within societies and within academia. *[Article copies available for a fee from The Haworth Document Delivery Service: 1-800-HAWORTH. E-mail address: <docdelivery@haworthpress.com> Website: <http://www.HaworthPress.com> © 2003 by The Haworth Press, Inc. All rights reserved.]*

KEYWORDS. Gloria Anzaldúa, Chicano Studies, mestiza (mestizaje), borderlands (frontera)

Alejandro Solomianski is currently an assistant professor at Cal State, Los Angeles. He obtained his PhD and MA at the University of Pittsburgh and his bachelor's degree at the Univerisity of Buenos Aires. He has taught at the University of Buenos Aires, a marginalized neighborhood in Buenos Aires known colloquially as "Fort Apache," and the University of Pittsburgh. He has published several academic articles, a book of poetry, and a play. This last work was performed at the Babilonia playhouse in Buenos Aires (1991) and in several venues by the Centro Cultural San Martín de Buenos Aires (most recently in August 2001). His academic interests center on the intersection of subaltern studies and Latin American colonial and postcolonial culture.

[Haworth co-indexing entry note]: "Moving *La Frontera* Towards a Genuine Radical Democracy in Gloria Anzaldúa's Work." Solomianski, Alejandro . Co-published simultaneously in *Journal of Lesbian Studies* (Harrington Park Press, an imprint of The Haworth Press, Inc.) Vol. 7, No. 3, 2003, pp. 57-72; and: *Latina Lesbian Writers and Artists* (ed: María Dolores Costa) Harrington Park Press, an imprint of The Haworth Press, Inc., 2003, pp. 57-72. Single or multiple copies of this article are available for a fee from The Haworth Document Delivery Service [1-800-HAWORTH, 9:00 a.m. - 5:00 p.m. (EST). E-mail address: docdelivery@haworthpress.com].

http://www.haworthpress.com/store/product.asp?sku=J155
© 2003 by The Haworth Press, Inc. All rights reserved.
10.1300/J155v07n03_05

Quinientos años
celebrando la matanza del indígena
¡No hay nada que festejar!

–Los Fabulosos Cadillacs

[Five centuries
celebrating the killing of the indigenous.
There is nothing to celebrate!]
The growing presence of women, and people of color in large cities
along with a declining middle class have facilitated the operation of
devalorization processes. . . . [T]here is a systemic relation between this
globalization and feminization of wage labor.

–Saskia Sassen

For it is always finally unclear what is meant by invoking the lesbian-
signifier.

–Judith Butler

The man now being actually supreme in the house. . . . This autocracy
was confirmed and perpetuated by the overthrow of mother right. . . . The
next step leads us to the upper stage of barbarism, the period when all
civilized peoples have their heroic age: the age of iron sword . . .

–Frederick Engels–Barbarism and Civilization
(*The Origin of the Family, Private Property and the State*)

READING AS AN EXPERIENCE AND THE EXPERIENCE
OF READING A "DIFFERENT" TEXT

The first time I had the opportunity to read the amazing text called *Border-
lands/La Frontera*, by Gloria Anzaldúa, was in a graduate seminar on Latino
and Latin-American narrative from the Boom to the Post-Boom (since the '60s
until the present) at a prestigious U.S. research university. The professor was a
renowned specialist on the work of the Latin American Nobel Prize winner
Miguel Angel Asturias and a very well recognized scholar on (and personal
friend of) Gabriel García Márquez. I consider this man to be not only a highly
qualified discussion moderator but also an independent thinker and a left-wing

utopian who had become disgusted with and critical of the postmodern status quo in 1997. There were twelve students in class, and only four women. I mention the space in which this reading, analysis and discussion took place because I believe it shows us clearly that the interpretative atmosphere was conditioned by male (or phallic) centered discursive strategies. Beyond a theoretical equality, I would say that involuntarily (i.e., in spite of whatever efforts were made by the group), ontological hierarchies based upon white male-heterosexual supremacy lingered and tainted our collective experience of reading. In the first place, the institutional space itself created a social demarcation through prestige and validation that the institution and the field of study offered. Additionally, both Miguel Angel Asturias and Gabriel García Márquez–whose works (legitimately, perhaps) made up a significant part of the course, as well as of the graduate reading list–are white male heterosexuals (though at least Latino) who have been "glorified" with Nobel Prizes. The different receptions of and reactions to *Borderlands* in this context are critically relevant and characterize several possible aesthetical-political positions. From this point of view, my first experience of reading *La Frontera* was carried out in a quite suggestive laboratory.

In this experimental reading space, there are at least three aspects (besides the genuine or original perception of the reader) that should be considered carefully. First, the highly competitive logic of the "communal" reading exercise confers a privilege (through the grading system used in the course) to private interpretation rather than to the "implicit reader" created by Gloria Anzaldúa in the text itself (it means to the "ideal collective reader" produced and presupposed by the ideology, meanings, idioms, and other particular characteristics of the text). Second, there is a mandatory, institutional pact in a classroom setting that demands a response to this book (as to the other books covered in the seminar). Third, these responses were public and exposed, not only an academic level, but also as a personal set of values.

As could be expected, the sessions devoted to *Borderlands/La Frontera* were the most uncertain and problematic for the class, meaning that the work was utterly successful: the opinions expressed were multiple, contradictory, and passionate, but not necessarily positive. I would say that this result sprang directly from the numerous virtues of her book: its revelations about limitations; its ambiguities and contradictions; the social and academic values it expresses.

There were three basic reactions to the book: (a) explicit repulsion; (b) agitated surprise and confusion; and (c) intense admiration. In any case, the text was never received with boredom or indifference. It was, however, the least venerated book of those covered in this seminar, and, because of that, also the most provocative. The text challenged our existential points of view. Even the seminar coordinator, an open-minded visionary, admitted, in a gesture of sincerity, that although he has a high regard for Anzaldúa's work, he cannot avoid feeling somewhat uncomfortable when he reads it. An irrational sensation, originating in internalized homophobia (considered by the reader himself unacceptable) that has permeated Western "reality," emerged as an involuntary response to the brave and defiant configuration of the book.

Some readers–those with a fondness for order and hierarchy, and who may even feel unconfident about their own sexual identities–shouted ultimately meaningless lectures about the transcendental and timeless values of the Western canon, the necessary demise of what they consider subproducts of the literary market, and the disgusting taste of some fashionable, elitist texts. In any case, these kinds of reactions are symptomatic of the very preconceptions and privileges that Gloria Anzaldúa questions, disrupts and puts at risk through her text.

In its most elemental aspect, *Borderlands/La Frontera* removes the solidness of the category "book." Its inquiring writing goes far beyond an acute and complex deconstruction of the boundaries among discursive and literary genres/genders. *Borderlands* ruins the ideological dominance of the artifact "book" through the complicity between oral and written discourses, through the oral and popular circulation of words and messages that emerges throughout the text. The constant mixing of popular songs and poetry with sometimes poetic prose problematizes the literary discourse. On the other hand, the choices of texts written by Violeta Parra, Alfonsina Storni or Gina Valdés (re)produce a feminist tradition that defines a peculiar Latina identity. Anzaldúa could have chosen to quote Sappho of Lesbos or Sor Juana Inés de la Cruz, but did not. Instead, she opted to emphasize–or (re)create–a Latina feminist tradition and to avoid the reappearance of an already prestigious Western-Lesbian heritage.

Carefully reading *Borderlands*, one perceives the sophisticated scaffolding of the text hidden behind an apparently naïve surface, a range of knowledge freely intended to appear rustic, a text configuration faked as weak, inexperienced, or even improvised. A serious and deep reading of the book reveals, together with its extreme complexity, the skillful aesthetic and ideological consciousness that Gloria Anzaldúa exercised to write it. I would propose that in her text there is no word, no tone, and no allusion that is randomly written.

From this point of view, one of the most relevant ways in which *Borderlands* questions the Eurocentric idea of the "book" and "literary discourse" is through its link to Amerindian textual traditions and its employment of anti-logocentric images and sensations:

> For the ancient Aztecs, *tlilli, tlapalli, la tinta negra y roja de sus códices* (the black and red ink painted on codices) were the colors symbolizing *escritura y sabiduría* (writing and wisdom). (Anzaldúa, 1987, 69)

Picking out images from my soul's eye, fishing for the right words to recreate the images. . . . *Escribo con la tinta de mi sangre.* I write in red. Ink.
(71)

To write, to be a writer, I have to trust and believe in myself as speaker,
as a voice for the images. . . . When I write it feels like I'm carving bone.
It feels like I'm creating my own face, my own heart–a Nahuatl concept.
(73)

What is striking about the writing process here is the continuous intertwin-
ing of English, Spanish and Nahuatl, along with the inclusion of several "dia-
lectal" variations of Spanish and the voluntary repetition of orthographic
"mistakes." The text practices and, at the same time, theorizes a radical equal-
ization or vindication of multiple codes of communication.

We are robbed of our female being by the masculine plural.
Language is a male discourse. . . . Even our own people, other
Spanish speakers *nos quieren poner candados en la boca.* They
Would hold us back with their bag of *reglas de academia.* (54)

But Chicano Spanish is a border tongue which developed naturally.
Change, *evolución, enriquecimiento de palabras nuevas por
invención o adopción* have created variants of Chicano Spanish,
un nuevo lenguaje. Un lenguaje que corresponde a un modo de vivir.
Chicano Spanish is not incorrect, it is a living language. (55)

This sociolinguist truth acts as a permanent democratizing earthquake
within a social space strongly determined by an unfair and asymmetric distri-
bution of power, social prestige and material (or even symbolic) resources.
Anzaldúa's treatment of the very raw materials that form the discursive text is the
starting point for a pretended naive critique of textual classifications and conventional discursive genres. A discursive genre, besides being the reenactment of a
tradition, is a hint or aid to the reader. It indicates what can be expected, the way
the narrative materials or images must be understood. Probably a small frac-
tion of the discomfort experienced by some readers in the aforementioned
graduate seminar came from this lack of culturally supported guidance. The
space of this seminar is epistemologically a very appropriate model for experiencing and analyzing the reading practice.

The first feeling when reading *Borderlands/La Frontera* is a sensation of
uncertainty because the old established values are not useful anymore if the
reader wants to access the meanings proposed by the text. From this perspec-

tive, it is a really striking experience of reading that demands an active and questioning reader prepared to doubt, to be open, to learn, and to change. The immediate textual fabric is a discourse that interweaves verse and prose,[1] high culture and popular culture references, historical written documents and oral familial memories, academic knowledge and folkloric wisdom. The text itself and its peculiar way of construction-deconstruction of meaning becomes, by virtue of its revolutionary functioning, a radically democratic space. Internally, there are no hierarchies, no sites of prestige or privilege, and no hegemonies. Careful study will show that Anzaldúa's work consciously exceeds a mere aesthetic exercise.

> The struggle has always been inner, and is played out in the outer terrains. Awareness of our situation must come before inner changes, which in turn come before changes in society. Nothing happens in the "real" world unless it first happens in the images in our heads. (87)

One of the problems that the prose of "Atravesando Fronteras/Crossing Borders" brought to the readers in the seminar was the genre labeling of the text. Were we reading a historical treatise or a family history? Was it a literary text or a scientific one?[2] Was it a testimony? Was it a collection of (not so well connected) academic papers? Was it a political manifesto?

In my opinion "Crossing Borders" is all those things at the same time; and what it is even more interesting: the text works voluntarily as a parody in order to represent all these genres in a defective way, saving some elements and condemning the male-colonized aspect of every genre in a gender hierarchical discourse (or in the society that it communicates and represents).

If we consider the category of testimony (testimonio) as proposed by John Beverley during the nineties,[3] we will find that, in Gloria Anzaldúa's case, the victim or "the other," in opposition to the established canon for this genre—which is based on Rigoberta Menchú's and Domitila Barrios de Chungara's testimonies—coincides completely with the figure of the "intellectual mediator." In spite of their differences, Menchu's and Barrios de Chungara's texts give voice to an Amerindian woman who learns horrible facts and denounces them from and as a collective (ethnic) experience. Therefore, these denunciations fundamentally have a communal value. In contrast, Anzaldúa's discourse has an individual value in its expression of anti-male dominance and anti-heterosexist experience.

If we approach each chapter as an academic account of a sociohistorical referent, or a particular system of relations, we will find immediately some discursive segments—for example, quotations from Mexican corridos or other popular songs—that would not—even in 2002, and much less in 1987—be deemed "appropriate academic sources" to corroborate the information presented by the text. The academic status quo is to label this type of writing naive or inexperienced, but there are elements that lead us to believe this is in fact a parody of "serious" academic discourse.

In the third chapter, "Entering into the Serpent," Anzaldúa deals in an intense way with different meanings, functions, and concepts of the referent "religion." This is certainly not a light subject for a Chicana lesbian thinker to be pondering.[4] The following is a very relevant and curious fragment in which Anzaldúa supposedly quotes a theoretical book to speak about the topic of religion:

> Institutionalized religion fears trafficking with the spirit world and stigmatizes it as witchcraft. It has strict taboo against this kind of inner knowledge. It fears what Jung calls the Shadow, the unsavory aspects of ourselves. But even more it fears the supra-human, the god in ourselves. "The purpose of any established religion–is to glorify, sanction and bless with superpersonal meaning all personal and interpersonal activities. This occurs through the 'sacraments' and indeed through most religious rites."[33] But it sanctions only its own sacraments and rites. Voodoo, Santeria, Shamanism and other native religions are called mythologies. In my own life, the Catholic Church fails to give meaning to my daily acts, to my continuing encounters with the "other world." It and other institutionalized religions impoverish all life, beauty, pleasure. (37)

After such a meaningful, sharp and serious accusation, the academic reader will go directly to note number 33 to find the source of such a clear formulation of the mechanisms of the religious institution. What one will find there, however, is this funny and ironic commentary: "33. I have lost the source of this quote. If anyone knows what it is, please let the publisher know" (95). Having completed my PhD in the United States, I know through personal experience that this note would be unacceptable in a final paper for a graduate course, and would be much more inappropriate in an academic text designed for publication. I would say PhD-granting institutions in the U.S. and academic publications have much to do with the "institution," its "rituals" and rules of "authorization" that the author is discussing, in both logical and practical ways. Of course, twelve years later (1999), when the second edition of *Borderlands* was published and an interesting introduction by Sonia Saldívar-Hull was added, nobody had yet found "the source of the quote."

In all this academic parody there is a subtle element that, in my opinion, extends the criticism much further: we should remember that, by coincidence, the number of the note referring to Catholic dogma, 33, is not only the age at which Catholics believe Christ died, but also a triple allusion to the central truth of the Catholic faith–the mystery of the Trinity. But the possible connotations of this joke go beyond religion itself to question the legitimacy of a male divinity, and maybe even Eurocentric high culture, if one remembers the age of Dante Alighieri's "autobiographical" character in another of the foundational books of Western culture (yet another male-centered monument).

Besides the wide openness and the genre indeterminacy of *Borderlands*, the feeling that I experienced most intensively since my first reading was a radical and essential freedom. The strong impression that, at least within the utopian space of the text, equality can be a reality, and it is still possible to cross the border to the space of the cultural otherness even in a mass-mediated world where the market seems to have invaded everything. Then, when it was my turn to speak in the graduate seminar, I made reference to this radical experience of freedom and to the joy of thinking that, if a book such as *Borderlands* had been written and had crossed las fronteras de la academia, at least potentially, the human world had a chance to be moved to a better place.

In the following section of my study, I will analyze the alternative constructions of history and geopolitics proposed by the book. In the conclusion, I will summarize the mestiza identity of a human Western culture (as if these roles were a destiny and not mere possibilities among others). It is quite obvious that if we could change our colonized perception of reality and replace it with a set of egalitarian principles, reality, and not only perception, would be different. From this perspective "Crossing Borders" can be thought of as a shout for freedom or as an immense "speech act" in the deepest and most intense sense: a communicative act that intends to change the world.[5]

> To articulate the past historically does not mean to recognize "the way it really was". . . . The danger affects both the content of the tradition and its receivers. The same threat hangs over both: that of becoming a tool of the ruling classes. . . . Only that historian will have the gift of fanning the spark of hope in the past who is firmly convinced that *even the dead* will not be safe from the enemy if he wins. And this enemy has not ceased to be victorious.
>
> —Walter Benjamin

WHEN HISTORY AND GEOPOLITICS WERE AND ARE OTHER

Gloria Anzaldúa published her book five years before the fifth centenary of the European invasion of what was henceforth denominated America. This event is euphemistically, and as an ideological constraint, commonly referred to as the "Discovery of America."[6] The critique of this cultural encounter that emerged during this anniversary was tremendously serious and deep, and would produce several new points of view. Among several original books (a suitable list would be really large, so I will mention only a pair directly related to *Borderlands*) are *1492: El encubrimiento del otro* [1492: Suppressing the Other] by Enrique Dussel (1992) and *La voz y su huella* [Voice and its Imprint] by Martin Lienhard (1990). These books examined subjects already treated (with more or less detail) by Gloria Anzaldúa.[7] Among the symbolic constructs that gave meaning to the fifth centenary (1992) would be the first publication in almost five centuries of the complete works of Fray Bartolomé de Las Casas. This enormous editorial effort (14 volumes) was funded mainly by the Spanish state, and was, in fact, the first time the greater part of this work (perhaps more than 90%) had ever been published. Fray Bartolomé's historical work is probably the most famous instance of a narrative alternative in opposition to the "official story."

One of the most amazing merits of the narrative voice in *Borderlands* is the exposition–maybe even the inauguration–of a new and different conception of American history. But this Copernican turn is more complex than a mere change or inversion in the place of perception of historical events. This account is not the replacement of the vision of the winners by the vision of the defeated. In all probability, in Anzaldúa's rendition the meaning of "winners" and "defeated" is no longer clear or evident, so that historical processes recuperate the dense complexity they have in reality.

One could think of several Copernican turns because Anzaldúa's site of enunciation simultaneously responds to a variety of subaltern identities in combat among themselves, but peacefully combined in a coherent persona. From this point of view the Amerindian "person of color" has to subsume her female space and accept her conflictive lesbian side. The astonishing fact when reading her story is the harmonious integrity, the apparent simplicity of the narrative. Maybe the ethical responsibility to be fair to a multiplicity of identities requires an unbiased text devoid of the artificial requirement to persuade the reader or provide a convenient symbolic order. Perhaps this insubordination to the narrative interests of whatever group generates a genuine history that is as near as possible to "the way it really was."

In *Borderlands*, all the oppressors and all the migrations are on the same ontological plane. In the author's sharp feminist approach, some anthropological changes within the same ethnic group constitute a major historical event with heavier relevance for the human identity than the European arrival itself. The following quote will make this primary contribution of Anzaldúa's work completely patent:

During the original peopling of the Americas, the first inhabitants migrated across the Bering Straits and walked south across the continent. The oldest evidence of humankind in the U.S.–the Chicanos' ancient Indian ancestors–was found in Texas and has been dated to 35000 B.C. In the Southwest United States archeologist have found 20,000-year-old campsites of the Indians who migrated through, or permanently occupied, the Southwest, Aztlán-land of the herons, land of the whiteness, the Edenic place of origin of the Azteca. In 1000 B.C., descendents of the original Cochise people migrated into what is now Mexico and Central America and became the direct ancestors of many of the Mexican people. (The Cochise culture of the Southwest is the parent culture of the Aztecs. The Uto-Aztecan languages stemmed from the language of the Cochise people.) The Aztecs (the Nahuatl word for people of Aztlán) left the Southwest in 1168 A.D. . . . The symbolic sacrifice of the serpent to the "higher" masculine powers indicates that the patriarchal order had already vanquished the feminine and matriarchal order in pre-Columbian America. (5)[8]

In her report, this crucial identity change produced before and independently of the European arrival has even more cultural relevance than the last one (whose most notorious aspect is genocide) and will explain the deepest causes of the "success" of the Spanish conquest. I will quote in extension her piercing explanations. Through them, we will obtain an interesting new interpretation of apparently immobile "truths," a version of the facts from a totally not Eurocentric and not phallic-centric position.

At the beginning of the 16th century, the Spaniards and Hernán Cortés invaded Mexico and, with the help of tribes that the Aztecs had subjugated, conquered it. Before the Conquest there were twenty-five million Indian people in Mexico and the Yucatán. Immediately after the Conquest, the Indian population had been reduced to under seven million. By 1650, only one-and-a-half-million pure blooded Indians remained. (5)

The male-dominated Azteca-Mexica culture drove the powerful female deities underground by giving them monstrous attributes and by substituting male deities in their place . . . (27)

Before the Aztecs became a militaristic, bureaucratic state where male predatory warfare and conquest were based on patri-lineal nobility, the principle of balanced opposition between the sexes existed. (31)

The changes that led to the loss of the balanced oppositions began when the Azteca, one of the twenty Toltec tribes, made the last pilgrimage from a place called Aztlán. The migrations south began about the year A.D. 820. Three hundred years later the advance guard arrived near Tula, the capital of the declining Toltec empire. (32)

The Aztec ruler, *Itzcatl* destroyed all the painted documents (books called codices) and rewrote a mythology that validated the wars of conquest and thus continued the shift from a tribe based on clans to one based on classes. (32)

In defiance of the Aztec rulers, the *macehuales* (the common people) continued to worship fertility, nourishment and agricultural female deities, those of crops and rain. . . . Nevertheless, it took less than three centuries for Aztec society to change from the balanced duality of their earlier times and from egalitarian traditions of a wandering tribe to those of a predatory state. The nobility kept the tribute, the commoner got nothing, resulting in a class split. The conquered tribes hated the Aztecs because of the rape of their women and the heavy taxes levied on them. The *Tlaxcalans* were the Aztec's bitter enemies and it was they who helped the Spanish defeat the Aztec rulers, who were by this time so unpopular with their own common people that they could not even mobilize the populace to defend the city. Thus the Aztec nation fell not because *Malinali* (*la Chingada*) interpreted for and slept with Cortés, but because the ruling elite had subverted the solidarity between men and women and between noble and commoner. (33-34)

This interpretation of the facts differs notably from those that resort to European technical or intellectual "superiority" to explain everything that happened during the invasion. At the end of these passages, Anzaldúa leaves utterly implicit that she is communicating with a Mexican male interlocutor. She does not even bother to reveal his name in an endnote; probably because he is a great celebrity, a Nobel Prize winner, a great authority that supposedly can establish what it is the "authentic" Mexican identity.[9] In "The Sons of La Malinche," from *The Labyrinth of Solitude* (1950), a book that is supposedly a profound and even self-critical investigation, Octavio Paz distributes roles, genealogies, and "true" characters in mapping the national Mexican identity. This text has become a classic, and its affirmations usually circulate with a low level of critique. I will quote a few lines in order to observe the different scopes and places of enunciation in the works of both writers:

If the *Chingada* is a representation of the violated Mother, it is appropriate to associate her with the Conquest, which was also a violation, not only in the historical sense but also in the very flesh of Indian women. The symbol of this violation is doña Malinche, the mistress of Cortés. It is true that she gave herself voluntarily to the conquistador, but he forgot her as soon as her usefulness was over. Doña Marina becomes a figure representing the Indian women who were fascinated, violated or seduced by the Spanish. . . . [T]he Mexican people have not forgiven La Malinche for her betrayal. (Paz 86)[10]

If only in a brief way, I would like to give at least an idea of the ideological inconveniences that *Borderlands* can provoke among the "more cultured" segments on the Mexican side of *La Frontera*, especially in relation to the unfriendly, treacherous and dangerous Anglo neighbors. "The U.S.-Mexican border *es una herida abierta* where the Third World grates against the first and bleeds" (3). Those are the words that start chapter one and put the subject of discussion (among other places) in a conflictive geopolitical field.[11]

Three books were very useful in helping me understand this problem. *When Corporations Rule the World* by David Korten (1995) is a penetrating study of the global economy during the last decade that explores the current logic of production and accumulation (it devotes some pages to the "maquiladoras"). *Globalization and Its Discontents* by Saskia Sassen (1998) proposes a more specific approach to the simultaneous processes of female immigration to the "First World" and access to offshore production as a key to the contemporary creation of surplus value. Finally, the interesting and debatable *Empire* by Michael Hardt and Antonio Negri sees in the immense flow of population from the "subordinate regions of the world"[12] to the "more dominant" ones a mechanism that will make possible a revolutionary change. For them, the popular demands of "global citizenship" could generate a deep transformation in the general conditions of existence.

> Residency papers for everyone means in the first place that all should have the full rights of citizenship in the country where they live and work. . . . Capital itself has demanded the increased mobility of labor power and continuous migrations across national boundaries. (Hardt and Negri 400)

In the geo-political scheme Gloria Anzaldúa reveals, *Empire*'s thesis is not contradicted, as Anzaldúa makes clear that her Chicana rights to citizenship are linked to an extended history of abuse that exemplifies the monstrous face of capitalism.

We comfort ourselves by believing that neonazis or "skinheads" comprise only a small minority of the population, without considering that individuals in high social and public positions are empowered by the very hatred of otherness (with its correlative love of ignorance) that these subgroups advocate, and that private property and hierarchies are the last refuges of a capitalism that can no longer show a human face.

TOWARDS A NEW MESTIZA CONSCIOUSNESS

Concluding, I will explain very briefly the possibility of a new human stage of consciousness that is the solution proposed by *Borderlands*. This highest level of humanity could harmoniously, through an intelligent integration of the conflictive differences (not by their elimination), conduct us to a more genuine and democratic existence.[13]

All human beings have, beneath the surface, a "mestizo" identity that can be denied, but somehow, by constitution and in a very more remarkable way, a lesbian is undeniably "mestiza." Gloria Anzaldúa perceives this fact intellectually and through personal experience. With complete lucidity, she makes of it the key tool of her sociopolitical proposal. By means of this "essential," defining trait of lesbian identity, she attributes to homosexuality a unique mediation capacity: a universal space of intersection. In the fragment that I will quote next she does not directly mention it, but throughout the book it becomes clear that lesbians have, by virtue of being female, the possibility of experiencing an even deeper and more galvanizing discrimination than male homosexuals (in fact, the focus of her book is on lesbian borderlands situations and it is subtitled *The New Metiza*–making reference to *una conciencia de mujer*, 77-).

> Being the supreme crossers of cultures, homosexuals have strong bonds with the queer white, Black, Asian, Native American, Latino, and with the queer in Italy, Australia and the rest of the planet. We come from all colors, all classes, all races, all time periods. Our role is to link people with each other–the Blacks with Jews with Indians with Asians with whites with extraterrestrials. (84-85)

To her universal party, where all humans are truly equal, even the oppressors are invited, as long as they decide not to continue in their shameful role.

Many feel that whites should help their own people rid themselves of race hatred and fear first. I, for one, choose to use my energy to serve as a mediator. I think we need to allow whites to be our allies. (85)

Probably most of these ideas are utopian and remain quite far from our present situation. However, I ask myself how it could possibly be demeaning to be utopian. Besides, as Gloria noted, nothing happens in the "real" world unless it first happens in the images in our heads.

NOTES

1. Because of the space limits on my reflections on *La Frontera*, I will focus on only the first part of the book, "Atravesando Fronteras/ Crossing Borders," without any consideration of the collection of poems (some of them eminently narrative) titled "Un Agitado Viento/ Ehécatl, the Wind."

2. The complexities presupposed in this small question are so numerous that I am not even going to try to develop them. Terms like "fiction," "sources and documentation," and "regimes of truth" bring up elemental questions.

3. I refer here to *Against Literature*, a book that seems to have imposed a clear definition of the term within North American academia. The contributions of René Jara, Hernán Vidal, Miguel Barnet, and Elzbieta Sklodowska (among a long list of worthwhile works) present other interesting articulations of the concept.

4. My personal reading of the profound substance of Anzaldúa's ideas is in part conditioned by a book written a short time later that studies the same problematic theme and has already been accepted as a classic in the field: *La colonización de lo imaginario* [Colonization of the Imaginary] by Serge Gruzinski (originally written in French in 1988).

5. John Austin's book, *How to Do Things with Words* is, academically speaking, a mandatory reference here.

6. This event has enormous cultural relevance and in Spanish is usually written with capital letters.

7. The previously mentioned work by Serge Gruzinski (and all his subsequent investigations) can be included in this list. I am not presupposing a web of reciprocal influences, but rather a widespread shift in paradigm.

8. Anzaldúa annotates all the necessary bibliographical support for the statements made here.

9. I owe to "Sexuality and Discourse: Notes From a Chicana Survivor" by Emma Pérez the identification of this "secret" discursive counterpart and a clearer and more confident approach to this problematic field. Also, although I did not use in a direct or practical way her profound annotations, the book *Writing from the Borderlands* by Carmen Cáliz-Montoro helped me to understand (or maybe to feel) more intensely Anzaldúa's poetry.

10. Even an account as limited and self-centered as that presented by Bernal Díaz del Castillo (see Rolena Adorno about this matter) provides a much more complex and nuanced portrait of Malinche.

11. Two years after the publication of *Borderlands*, García Canclini, an intellectual consistently and substantially funded by the Mexican Government and other prestigious in-

stitutions, published *Culturas Híbridas* (1989). His book immediately became an acclaimed success and won the "Iberoamericano Book Award" of the Latin American Studies Association as the best book on Latin American studies for the period 1990-1992. His vision of the border could not be more opposed to Anzaldúa's. Canclini considers Tijuana, together with New York City, one of the biggest laboratories of "Postmodernity" and enthusiastically admires the population growth (from 60,000 in 1950 to a million in 1990). This perplexingly admiring picture of Tijuana can be found on pages 293 to 305 in the book referenced in my bibliography.

12. The authors do not accept the analytical categories of "First" and "Third World."

13. A summary of all the formal-academic discussions about lesbian identity would exceed my space limits. What these essentially deduce, is that it is as absurd to propose a common gay or lesbian identity as it is to propose a common heterosexual identity. The distances between the queerness of "people of color" and the queerness of the privileged segments of society are patent. No identity (ethnic, cultural, sexual, age) will guarantee a humane coexistence or the respect for otherness that would resolve social conflicts. The article "Fighting the Gay Right" by Richard Goldstein is very illustrative of this point. Some other texts that helped me to have a clearer idea on the perspectives and conflicts of this problematic field are "Performing 'La Mestiza': Lesbians of Color Negotiating Identities" by Ellen M. Gil-Gomez, *The Truth that Never Hurts* by Barbara Smith, "Irigaray's Female Symbolic in the Making of Chicana Lesbian *Sitios y Lenguas*" by Emma Pérez, "Inverts and Hybrids: Lesbian Rewritings of Sexual and Racial Identities" by Judith Raiskin, *Representation: Cultural Representations and Signifying Practices* by Stuart Hall, and *The Racial Contract* by Charles Mills.

WORKS CITED

Adorno, Rolena. "Discourses on Colonialism: Bernal Díaz, Las Casas, and the Twentieth Century Reader." *MLN,* 103-2, Hispanic Issue (Mar. 1988): 239-258.

Anzaldúa, Gloria. *Borderlands. La Frontera.* San Francisco: Aunt Lute Books, 1987.

Austin, John. *How to Do Things with Words.* Oxford: Oxford University Press, 1962.

Barrios de Chungara, Domitila. Viezzer, Moema (ed.) *"Si me permiten hablar. . . ." México: siglo xxi editors, 1978.*

Beverley, John. *Against Literature.* Minneapolis and London: University of Minnesota Press, 1993.

Cáliz-Montoro, Carmen. *Writing from the Borderlands.* Toronto: TSAR Publications, 2000.

Díaz del Castillo, Bernal. *Historia verdadera de la Conquista de la Nueva España.* México: Porrúa, 1994.

Dussel, Enrique. *1492: El encubrimiento del otro.* Bogotá: Antropos, 1992.

García Canclini, Nestor. *Culturas híbridas.* México: Grijalbo, 1990.

Gil-Gomez, Ellen. "Performing 'La Mestiza': Lesbians of Color Negotiating Identities." Griffin, Gabriele (ed.) *'Romancing the Margins'? Lesbian Writing in the 1990s.* New York. London.Oxford: Harrington Park Press, 2000 (21-38).

Goldstein, Richard. "Fighting the Gay Right." *The Nation,* July 1, 2002.

Hall, Stuart. *Representation. Cultural Representations and Signifying Practices.* London: Sage, 1997.

Hardt, Michael and Negri, Antonio. *Empire*. Cambridge and London: Harvard University Press, 2000.

Jara, René and Vidal, Hernán (ed.). *Testimonio y Literatura*. Minneapolis: Institute For The Study Of Ideologies And Literatures, 1986.

Korten, David. *When Corporations Rule the World*. West Hartford and San Francisco: Kumarian Press and Berret-Koehler Publishers, 1996.

Lienhard, Martin. *La voz y su huella*. La Habana: Casa de las Américas, 1990.

Menchú, Rigoberta and Burgos-Debray Elisabeth (ed.). *Me llamo Rigoberta Menchú y así me nació la conciencia*. México: siglo xxi, 1985.

Mills, Charles. *The Racial Contract*. Ithaca and London: Cornell University Press, 1997.

Paz, Octavio. *The Labyrinth of Solitude*. New York: Grove Press, 1985.

Pérez, Emma. "Sexuality and Discourse: Notes From a Chicana Survivor." Alarcón, Norma, Castro Rafaela and others (eds.), *Chicana Critical Issues*. Berkeley: Third Woman Press, 1993 (45-69).

_____. "Irigaray's Female Symbolic in the making of Chicana *Sitios y Lenguas*." Laura Doan (ed.), *The Lesbian Postmodern*. New York: Columbia University Press, 1994 (104-117).

Raiskin, Judith. "Inverts and Hybrids: Lesbian Rewritings of Sexual and Racial Identities." Laura Doan (ed.), *The Lesbian Postmodern*. New York: Columbia University Press, 1994 (156-172).

Sassen, Saskia. *Globalization and Its Discontents*. New York: The New Press, 1998.

Sklodowska, Elzbieta. *Testimonio hispanoamericano*. New York: Peter Lang, 1992.

Smith, Barbara. *The Truth That Never Hurts*. New Brunswick, New Jersey, and London: Rutgers University Press, 1988.

llustration by Jennifer Whiting

Como Sabes, Depresión

H. Briana Levine

FIVE SENSES OF DEPRESSION: COMO ERES TÚ

I

I do no more shouting,
not any more;

I do no more calling out,
not any more;

I do no more talking,
not any more;

I do no more murmuring,
not any more;

I do no more whispering,
not any more.

H. Briana Levine is a sophomore majoring in Spanish and minoring in sociology at Smith College in Northampton, Massachusetts. She was born and raised in Allentown, Pennsylvania, and has also lived in Mexico and traveled extensively in Latin America. Although ideologically apposed to T.S. Eliot, she is inspired by his poetry. The most common themes in her writing are existentialism and her experience with clinical depression.

[Haworth co-indexing entry note]: "Como Sabes, Depresión." Levine, H. Briana. Co-published simultaneously in *Journal of Lesbian Studies* (Harrington Park Press, an imprint of The Haworth Press, Inc.) Vol. 7, No. 3, 2003, pp. 75-77; and: *Latina Lesbian Writers and Artists* (ed: María Dolores Costa) Harrington Park Press, an imprint of The Haworth Press, Inc., 2003, pp. 75-77. Single or multiple copies of this article are available for a fee from The Haworth Document Delivery Service [1-800-HAWORTH, 9:00 a.m. - 5:00 p.m. (EST). E-mail address: docdelivery@haworthpress.com].

http://www.haworthpress.com/store/product.asp?sku=J155
10.1300/J155v07n03_06

Now that I am silent
you somehow still follow me, even more easily,
and I hear you.

II

You know my lengua.
Rolling around in my mouth,
looking for sweet,
she got a lick of sour metal on her canker sores,
(there once was blood there)
but found a sugar spot behind a molar–
from the remnants of a cracker.

She tastes salt when you trickle down my face;
bitter only 'till my cheek is (raw) clean.

III

With a soft kiss you take me.
When you caress me
your finger nails sting red lines on the
undersides of my arms.
However cold my skin my face
my hands your hands send them a chill.

If all those body parts catch frostbite
they will have to be removed.
I would lose the sensation of your touch and
you would have no place to grip and pin me
down.
Pero ya no habría nada de mí.

IV

Nobody else can see you.
I could be imagining your presence.
Sometimes you leave tracks so I
will not be the only one in your audience,
the only one to appreciate your handiwork.
You try to trick me into thinking I am your

one and only, the only one you see.
Sometimes I know better.

When everyone is watching
I want you here for validation.
When no one is looking
I want you gone.

V

Carbon Monoxide: a colorless odorless gas.
Deadly too.

You have never worn a signature scent,
but I smell you anyway:
in acetaminophen, the vodka
and a shard of glass;
in the purge bile, my cry tears
and my cutting blood.
I know you have been there.
Your musk stays with me
because you are still here, inside me,
even now.
Ya hueles como yo.

To Sor Juana

Mary L. Díaz

First feminist of the Americas,
champion in defending my right to know.
Destroyed, resurrected, reconstructed.
Notoriety and celebration,
Sor Filotea,
determination and moral courage
were not enough to keep you
in your rightful place.
Peor de todas,
mejor que casi todas.

In the confines of your convent,
Enduring the rules of men.
Religious order.
Irreligious orders.
Undermined by those you trust and respect.
Exploited for your talents and abilities.
Days and nights reading and writing
within the privilege of your confinement.

Mary L. Díaz is a licensed clinical social worker and psychotherapist. She received her EdD at Claremont Graduate School, her MA at San Diego State University, and her BA at California State University, Northridge. She has given numerous presentations to groups working with Latinas (and other women) on such issues as stress management, eating disorders, and self-esteem.

[Haworth co-indexing entry note]: "To Sor Juana." Díaz, Mary L. Co-published simultaneously in *Journal of Lesbian Studies* (Harrington Park Press, an imprint of The Haworth Press, Inc.) Vol. 7, No. 3, 2003, pp. 79-85; and: *Latina Lesbian Writers and Artists* (ed: María Dolores Costa) Harrington Park Press, an imprint of The Haworth Press, Inc., 2003, pp. 79-85. Single or multiple copies of this article are available for a fee from The Haworth Document Delivery Service [1-800-HAWORTH, 9:00 a.m. - 5:00 p.m. (EST). E-mail address: docdelivery@ haworthpress.com].

http://www.haworthpress.com/store/product.asp?sku=J155
10.1300/J155v07n03_07

Freedom is not without consequence.
Demoralized, subjugated, betrayed.
What led them to destroy a brilliant woman?
Jealousy? Envy? Ambition? Control?
Why your downfall, Juana Inés?

Unsupported, targeted for damnation
from those devoted to God.
For your delightful expression,
pride of the convent,
disdained and disrupted.

You upset their minds,
you upset my mind.

Under the rule of Spain,
under the rule of the king,
under the rule of Mexico,
under the rule of the Viceroy,
under the rule of the Archbishop,
under the rule of Catholicism,
under the old rule,
under unhappy rule,
under disbelieving power.

Foolish men accuse.
Foolish men without reason.
Foolish men do not forgive
beauty, passion, talent,
bordellos,
convents,
freedom.

Behind cell bars,
demanding of you obedience,
urgent circumstances,
veils, chastity,
weakness,
vulnerability,
the place of woman beneath man,
retreat.

They will change the rules
to vindictiveness,
sabotage,
secrecy,
offense.

They forbid you your work,
your love,
your anger,
your pride,
your personal hell.

They who will not sit with women,
even smart women,
but never hesitate to quote them.
They who avoid direct conflict
by hiding behind hierarchy.
They who do not know enough
to mix theology with philosophy.
They who have never confessed to you
their admiration of your brilliance,
of your beauty.

Your love, though, begins
with apprehension,
in solitude,
with ardor,
with danger and fear,
and sleeplessness.

Surrounded by their vanities,
you put God in the passion of your verses
which they dismissed as invalid.

You want to study,
to be protected by the convent walls,
to not be admonished for your affections.

Perverse?
Lascivious?
Morbid sensuality?

Exalting another woman?
Distasteful?

Sor Filotea,
thank you for not being more careful,
thank you for your letters,
your gospel,
your genius,
your reading,
your vile news of the earth,
your refutations of distinguished theologians,
your likings,
your preferences,
your defenses.

Thank you for your confessions,
your betrayal,
the aggression you endured.

Thank you for your judgment,
your conflict,
your justice,
your trial.

You reveal your awareness in your disguise,
your abominated state,
your sex,
your first dream.

All of it condemned,
defied, defiant
digressions, scribblings.

You defend me in your fury.
Your unbecoming amorous poems
become my state.
Never stop your scribbling.
Never stop learning.
Never stop writing.

I was wronged when you were wronged.
I failed when you failed.
I was reprimanded when you were reprimanded.
They do not trust the sound judgment of women.

You and all Mexican women are instruments,
desires, ends,
assigned to men by law and moral codes
on which we're not consulted.
Prostitutes, goddesses,
repositories, images of male energies,
reflections of their desires.

We experience your rage.
We are told in your conviction.
We learn from your tireless efforts.
We know from your persecution.
We are holy in your moment of triumph.
We understand in your beauty.
We are discredited in your confession.

If you were not a woman, it would not matter.
If we were not women, we would not matter.

God created women to philosophize,
to be impertinent,
to respond,
to create,
to reveal,
to call men bastards when they will not listen,
to yell–ENOUGH!
to be different,
to leave the convent,
to be the devil for the confessor,
to love countesses,
to guide,
to have literary ambitions,
to excel,
to die.

God created Mexican women
for glory,
for accolades,
for symbolic meanings
and loving bonds among women.
Not for marriage
and decent things.
Not for waiting.

God created Mexican women
to be challenged,
but not humbly,
not passively,
not suffering.

God created us to devour books,
to gain dreadful reputations as learned women,
to have first loves
and have our hearts broken.

God created us for amorous torment,
for craving,
melancholy.

God made us to remove our veils,
to look deeply,
reach out and touch a face,
to kiss gently.

This Juana is God's.
The Queen's. Mine.
Mexico's.
Spain's.

First dream.
Nearer to God.
Worthy creature.
I write your name,
Juana Inés,
the best of all.

Your dignity continues to live
in the writings of Hispanic women.
Your will can be read
in the letters of lesbian poets.

Your ultimate triumph
is the greatest love poem.

NOTE

Inspired by the film *Yo, la peor de todas (I the Worst of All)*. Directed by María Luisa Bemberg. First Run/Icarus Films, 1990.

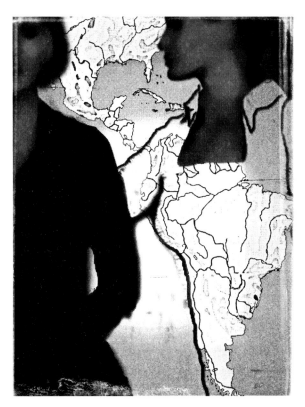

Illustration by Tonya López-Craig

Lesbianism and Caricature
in Griselda Gambaro's *Lo impenetrable*

Ignacio López-Calvo

SUMMARY. This article explores the work of novelist Griselda Gambaro as a lesbian discourse that counters the prevailing patriarchal discourse of the Latin American dictatorships. Gambaro's work is placed in the context of other Latin American "lesbian" texts that also challenge the political status quo by providing deviant models of female sexuality. *[Article copies available for a fee from The Haworth Document Delivery Service: 1-800- HAWORTH. E-mail address: <docdelivery@haworthpress.com> Website: <http://www.HaworthPress. com> © 2003 by The Haworth Press, Inc. All rights reserved.]*

Ignacio López-Calvo was born in Segovia, Spain, in 1968. He received his undergraduate degrees in English and French from Universidad Complutense, Madrid, and his master's and PhD degrees in Romance Languages from the University of Georgia, and is currently Associate Professor of Spanish at California State University, Los Angeles. His fields of specialization are Latin American Southern Cone narrative and Literary Theory. He is the author of two books, *Written in Exile. Chilean Fiction from 1973-Present* (New York: Routledge, 2001) and *Religión y militarismo en la obra de Marcos Aguinis 1963-2000* (New York: Edwin Mellen Press, 2002), as well as over thirty articles and book chapters on Latin American and Spanish literature and culture in journals such as *Revista Iberoamericana, Cuadernos Americanos, Alba de América, Confluencia, Francographies, Revista Interamericana, La Torre,* and *Cuadernos de ALDEEU.* López-Calvo is currently writing the book *'Trujillo and God': Literary Representations of the Dominican Dictator,* which will be published in 2004. He has also given thirty-seven presentations in professional conferences in Europe, Latin America, and the United States.

[Haworth co-indexing entry note]: "Lesbianism and Caricature in Griselda Gambaro's *Lo impenetrable.*" López-Calvo, Ignacio. Co-published simultaneously in *Journal of Lesbian Studies* (Harrington Park Press, an imprint of The Haworth Press, Inc.) Vol. 7, No. 3, 2003, pp. 89-103; and: *Latina Lesbian Writers and Artists* (ed: María Dolores Costa) Harrington Park Press, an imprint of The Haworth Press, Inc., 2003, pp. 89-103. Single or multiple copies of this article are available for a fee from The Haworth Document Delivery Service [1-800-HAWORTH, 9:00 a.m. - 5:00 p.m. (EST). E-mail address: docdelivery@haworthpress.com].

10.1300/J155v07n03_08

KEYWORDS. Griselda Gambaro, Argentine literature, Southern Cone narrative, lesbianism in Latin American literature, Latin American dictatorship

Maguer que nos agravia de fablar en cosa que es muy sin guisa de cuidar, è muy sin guisa de facer; pero porque mal pecado alguna vez aviene, que home codicia à otro por pecar con él contra natura: mandamos, que qualesquier que sean, que tal pecado fagan, que luego que fuere sabido, que amos à dos sean castrados ante todo el pueblo, è despues, à tercer dia, sean colgados por las piernas fasta que mueran, è nunca dende sean tollidos. (Las Siete Partidas de Alfonso X el Sabio)

(Although it bothers us to talk about something unpleasant to consider or to do, but because at times such a sin actually takes place, that a man wants another and sins with him contra natura: we order that, no matter who they are that commit such a sin, that after finding out about it, that both be castrated before the whole town, and afterward, on the third day, they be hung by the legs until they die without being crippled. [Alphonse X the Wise's *Las Siete Partidas*])

The military coups of the 1960s and 1970s that stormed Latin America with their so-called national security regimes created a sort of continental pan-dictatorship that often attempted to impose its conservative moral views about sexuality on the citizenry. Inevitably, this new attitude affected cultural production either through the authors' self-censorship or through the origination of new ways to evade official censorship within the national borders. Paradoxically, at the same time that these regimes dictated morality and manipulated social habits they commonly practiced indiscriminate sexual violence when they tortured political prisoners in crowded prisons. In those enclosed quarters it became unnecessary to continue the hypocritical morality advertised by the juntas' discourses, and rape became a way to "extricate the national cancer" and fight "the international communist conspiracy." In this context, Fernando Reati exposes such contradictions and explores its reflection in literary discourses:

The use of sexual perversion as a metaphor would be the result of the violence that society itself encourages, insofar as the writer becomes a channel of expression of the same discourse that he is denouncing, a subject-object of the aberration constituted by his themes. In a patriarchal and authoritarian society the only kind of exacerbated pleasure is perversion, and the authors canalize that perverse aggression through their writing. (232)[1]

During the Argentine "Dirty war" gays and lesbians were particularly perse-cuted–more so than in the neighboring dictatorship under Augusto Pinochet–and homosexuality was often presented as a crime, an anomaly, a deviation, or a disease. Literature, then, echoed the fact that the victims' bodies had become passive objects of humiliation and torment, a mirror of political struggle, and a metaphorical text in which military victory had to be inscribed. The traditionally negative connotations ascribed to the human body, in particular to the female body, as well as the condemnation of active homosexuality by the Catholic Church, plausibly allowed the new repressive attitude to become more accept-able to Latin American societies. Consequently, the connection between power, discourse, gender, sexuality, and sexual violence became a common topic in nu-merous Latin American novels. The lesbian presence and the roles played by lesbians not only in Latin American communities but also in the authors' imag-ery have been represented in Latin American literature in variegated ways. Along with the defense of a tolerant attitude toward sexual orientation, many works reflect the universal social criticism that denounces gender inequalities and the ancestral frustration of women whose voices have been traditionally silenced. Others, however, evolve to more subversive expressions and attempt to scandalize the reader through the defiance of patriarchy and the transgres-sion of the social codes of sexual morality. The representation of lesbianism in Southern Cone narratives has a limited but consistent tradition. Considering contemporary Chilean novel, for example, in *The Obscene Bird of Night* (*El obsceno pájaro de la noche*; 1970) by José Donoso (1924-96) there are scenes of lesbianism among a group of old ladies in a nursing home that challenge pa-triarchal conventions, even though they are restricted to childlike games. In the same vein, in *La misteriosa desaparición de la marquesita de Loria* (The Mys-terious Disappearance of the Marquise of Loria; 1980) Donoso presents the re-lationship between three women, Tere Castillo, Casilda, and Blanca, who become involved in a *ménage à trois* with the Count of Almanza and defend their lesbianism as an alternative way of life that must be accepted by society.

Moving along to a younger generation of Chilean writers, in his collection of chronicles *Loco afán. Crónicas de sidario* (Crazy Zeal. AIDS Diary Chroni-cles; 1996), Pedro Lemebel (1950) acknowledges the help provided by celeb-rities such as Liz Taylor, Liza Minnelli, Barbra Streisand, and María Félix to gay men infected with AIDS, at the same time that he questions their negli-gence towards lesbians in the same situation. In addition, in a chronicle enti-tled "Las Amazonas de la Colectiva Lésbica Feminista Ayuquelén," included in *De perlas y cicatrices. Crónicas radiales* (Of Pearls and Scars. Radio

Chronicles; 1996), Lemebel celebrates the combative attitude of this feminist lesbian association as it struggled for tolerance during Pinochet's dictatorship and attempted to dignify the lifestyle of the women of the group, but he laments the fact that "sexual love among women is more repressed in these systems where sometimes gays serve as a flower vase in the euphoric neo-liberal celebration" (156).[2] In the end, they are expelled from the feminist Casa de la Mujer La Morada, and one of their leaders, Mónica Briones, who rebels against the macho attitude in a bar, becomes a symbol for the movement after she is lynched by a mob.

Alternative representations of lesbianism can also be observed in the works of Chilean Isabel Allende and in novels by Argentine women writers, such as *Mal don* (Bad Deal; 1973) by Silvia Bullrich, *Cama de ángeles* (Bed of Angels; 1983) by Alina Diaconú, *En breve cárcel* (In a Small Prison; 1989) by Sylvia Molloy, *Monte de venus* (Mount of Venus; 1976) by Reina Roffé, *Conversación al sur* (*Mothers and Shadows*; 1981) by Marta Traba, *La condesa sangrienta* (The Bloody Countess; 1965) by Alejandra Pizarnik, and *Lo impenetrable* (*The Impenetrable Madam X*; 1984) by Griselda Gambaro. Thus, in Allende's *The House of the Spirits* (*La casa de los espíritus*; 1982) we have a well-rounded lesbian character in Férula, Esteban Trueba's sister, who feels sexually attracted to Clara, her sister-in-law. Férula loves taking care of her and is tempted to sleep with her in order to feel her presence. Soon, Férula feels extremely jealous of her brother Esteban, who, suspecting that she is perverting his wife and ruining his marriage, expels her from the house after he sees the two women sleeping together. Later on, however, Férula will return in the shape of a ghost to show the depth of her love for Clara even after death.

As to the works by Argentine authors, *La condesa sangrienta* (The Bloody Countess; 1965) by Pizarnik (1936-72) provides a totally different vision of lesbianism in literature, relating it to sadism, insanity, torture, death, voyeurism, and sexual perversion. It explores the life of Erzébet Báthonry, "a noblewoman who tortured and killed over six hundred young women in sexual rituals associated with the search for eternal youth" (Altamiranda 332). In a completely different atmosphere, *Mothers and Shadows* by Marta Traba (1930-83) displays a potential lesbian relationship between two women of different generations, Dolores and Irene, which is eventually frustrated by intolerant social conventions and the violence of the Dirty war. After the regime's police break into the house, the two women are kidnapped and presumably "disappear." While adverse circumstances prevent a sexual relationship between the two women, the conversations that they hold transcend physical desire to reach a level of communication that is profoundly beneficial for both of them. Existential angst had turned the protagonists' lives into a sort of limbo, but they begin to make sense again once they come to the conclusion that the efforts of the past have not been in vain and that they are not alone in the struggle.

Solidarity, commitment, empathy, trust, as well as both oral and written language become tools for resistance and a refuge for survival. This is precisely the optimistic side of an otherwise pessimistic novel, if we consider the tragic denouement of the plot. With the backdrop of the demonstrations by the mothers of the disappeared at the Plaza de Mayo, which are blatantly ignored by the military dictatorship, a patriarchal morality stops Irene from hugging and expressing her love to Dolores. For the same reason, during a train trip to the south of the country, Dolores does not dare confess her feelings to Victoria, one of the leaders of the Buenos Aires resistance. The possibility of a lesbian relationship is presented in *Mothers and Shadows* as an appeal for plurality and freedom of sexual identity (as a synecdoche of freedom in general) during those times when monolithic homogeneity was the unattainable official goal. As Foster suggests, "perhaps the best way of seeing these texts as contributions toward a Latin American discourse of sexuality is in terms of their variegated challenges to compulsory heterosexuality" (*Cultural Diversity* 70). Mothers, in particular, become the victims of terror, political repression, and violence in the novel: while Dolores loses her baby as a result of having been kicked by torturers when she was pregnant, Irene's son and the daughter of Irene's friend, Elena, have disappeared. But the criticism of patriarchal codes of conduct goes beyond the junta's atrocities when Dolores visualizes her mother's honeymoon as mere rape: "even worse to imagine her on her honeymoon. What a stupid name for pure rape!" (94-5).[3] Like in Manuel Puig's *The Kiss of the Spider Woman* (*El beso de la mujer araña*; 1976), political injustice and intolerance run parallel to sexual injustice and intolerance in Marta Traba's novel.

Like Marta Traba's *Mothers and Shadows*, *The Impenetrable Madam X* by Griselda Gambaro (1928) explores sexual frustration in lesbian relationships, albeit with a formulation that is to all intents and purposes different in tone and genre. During the military dictatorship of General Jorge Rafael Videla, Griselda Gambaro's novel *Ganarse la muerte* (Making a Death; 1976) was forbidden, as it was deemed a danger against social order and the institution of family. As a consequence, the author self-exiled in Barcelona, where she wrote *The Impenetrable Madam X* hoping to win an erotic novel contest, "La sonrisa vertical" (The Vertical Smile), created by Tusquets, a Spanish publisher. In the author's own words, she also conceived it as a therapeutic way to escape the dense atmosphere of her previous novel as well as the mental burden of the dictatorship in her country. Emulating Cervantes' attempt with *Don Quixote* to put an end to the tales of chivalry that were so popular at the time through the mockery of the conventions and common places of the genre, Gambaro admittedly tries to create a humorous remake, a parody of the clichés of the erotic novel as male fantasy. According to the author, when she finally returned to Argentina at the end of the eighties, she decided not to try publishing her work for two reasons: first, it would have been censured; second, its tone did not belong in the oppressive climate of the times. Three years later, however, she changed her mind, as she confesses on the back cover of the Torres Agüero edition: "Perhaps because now, after so much pain, it is possible to approach literature as a place of amusement, a place where the imagination, freedom from care, and unholyness, are little contributions to a more ludic and permissive society."[4]

The Impenetrable Madam X is very different from the rest of Gambaro's narrative production, since its imaginary context escapes the Argentine historical referent present in novels such as *Ganarse la muerte* (Earning a Death; 1976), *Dios no nos quiere contentos* (God Does Not Want Us to Be Happy; 1979), and *Después del día de fiesta* (After the Holiday; 1994). Instead, it constitutes an alternative representation of sexuality that transgresses traditional gender borders and stands as a challenge to patriarchal understandings of gender relations as well as the canons of the erotic novel written by and for men. The protagonist of this affected erotic novel is a twenty-seven-year-old woman (considered–according to the narrative voice–nearly old in those times) called Madam X, as she has forgotten her own name. She is an eccentric Spanish aristocrat of a past century that constantly postpones an emotional relationship with her maid and lover Marie in order to pursue a sexual relationship with an elusive and mysterious gentleman, whose name, Jonathan, we learn later in the account. For most of the narration, the protagonist hides behind the excuse of an unbridgeable class and gender barrier and acts in denial of her own sexual and emotional attachment to Marie: "she knows and accepts that there can be no contact whatsoever between us, not the slightest relationship because apart from social differences, there is an insurmountable barrier of sexual identity" (46).[5] As a consequence, perhaps to compensate her unconscious desire to have an emotional relationship with her servant, Madam X spoils her and allows her to regularly misbehave, disobey, and even pinch and insult her. Concurrently with this secret urge, she enjoys being allured by the voluptuous letters of her wooer, a man whose penis (which he ridiculously names his "mast") allegedly has extraordinary sexual powers.

Foreshadowing the last chapter of the novel, one day Madam X finds herself dreaming about Marie, instead of Jonathan. In the dream, Marie is a figure with both feminine and masculine attributes, who can transform herself at her will from a woman into a man and vice versa. The protagonist has to confess that she enjoys the variety exhibited by the oneiric figure and underscores the fact that neither type of body had disappointed her. Still in self-denial, Madam

X chooses to dismiss the dream as a simple nightmare and even considers scolding Marie for intruding her dreams without her permission. Unaware that for Madam X "the gentleman's charm was in his prodigious mast" (137),[6] Jonathan, on their last date, makes the mistake of explaining to her that she no longer needs to fear his phallus, as it has unmistakably lost the impetus of other times. Ultimately, to Madam X's detriment, Jonathan expresses–moments before dying–his profound satisfaction upon realizing that the mystery, and not the consummation of the sexual act, is what he enjoys the most: "Thank you, my God! Now I understand! [. . .] That which is impenetrable is the source of all pleasure because there is no pleasure without the unknown" (142-3).[7] These sentences come to explain the title of Griselda Gambaro's novel. Once and for all, as his inevitable premature ejaculation continues to prevent the long-announced climax, all of Jonathan's sexual promises are irrevocably exposed as a sham. For too many years, a ludicrous Madam X has been daydreaming about the upcoming sexual encounter with the supposedly vigorous and virile seducer. Now, she finally realizes that she has wasted the best days of her life looking forward to meeting a man that is more interested in fantasies and fetishes (like eating her handkerchief) than in having actual sexual intercourse with her.

Although jaded by disappointment, Madam X expresses her relief about seeing the end of the gentleman's "siege." Then, she turns her head to Marie, smells her, and calls her "criatura" (creature), the same term of endearment that Jonathan would use with her both in his letters and in person. Marie, in return, kisses her neck. Subsequently, there is an ambiguous paragraph that allows contrasting interpretations. A priori, it seems that Madam X feels so indignant with Jonathan that, in a sudden change in the direction of her sexual desire, she not only insults him but also states, along with Marie, her desire to degrade and penetrate him, as revenge against his blatant imposture. Somehow, the sexual violence of anal rape is presented as a way to underscore Marie's victory and domination over her relentless competition. In a way, with that sadistic impulse to sodomize Jonathan, she seeks to repair and alleviate the emotional damages caused by him:

> Their waists joined, they leapt over the gentleman's body, which had fallen to one side of the bed; and like so many times before but this time with a conscious joy that exalted and mutually illuminated them, amused and confident, they decided to delve into each other, to enjoy what was possible. To penetrate it. (145)[8]

In the original Spanish version of the novel Gambaro ends this passage with the pronoun "lo," "penetrarlo," which seemingly makes reference to Jonathan.

Yet, contrary to our interpretation, Evelyn Picon Garfield chooses to translate it as "to penetrate it"; that is, "lo" is understood as "it," instead of "him." In that case the exegesis of this scene would have to be completely different.

Making an implicit reference to the habits of today's society, the parodic narration of the adventures of this love triangle is sporadically interrupted by reflective segments in which the omniscient narrative voice condemns–more or less seriously–different social and sexual habits of the protagonist's times. In addition, the chapters are preceded by a series of theoretical premises about the erotic novel that reappear in the index at the end of the novel, making the text more self-reflective. Significantly, Picon Garfield's English translation substitutes the Spanish word "Índice" with "Instruction for writing an erotic novel" (147). These postulates explain the reasons why Gambaro was unable to approach the erotic genre canonically and had to choose, instead, a carnivalesque approach.

At the same time, these premises somewhat justify different aspects of the plot, including the irreverent scenes that bring it close to pornography. Thus, we learn that it is more appropriate to suggest risqué scenes than to include an excessive number of them, but there must be a strong and descriptive passage to let the imagination rest. Another postulate maintains that in an erotic novel it is common when sexual intercourse occurs due to the characters' inadvertence: "As in a painting, they act like *trompe l'oeils*, and within the story's plot they have no other significance" (83).[9] In this context, Marie does not miss an opportunity to go under Madam X's skirt or to initiate flirtation and sexual games. Faser de Zambrano underscores her relevant role:

> As a marginal figure who speaks and acts in a defiant way, she succeeds in reconfiguring the Columbine discourse defined by gender difference and sustained by compulsory heterosexuality, through a combative stratagem: lesbianization. (128)[10]

Similarly, the nurse at the hospital tries to alleviate Jonathan by sleeping with him, before she ends up having sex with five men at a time. Better than any other maxim, however, the following one justifies writing such an apparently trivial novel in those tumultuous times by indicating the therapeutic value of this type of literature: "Like eroticism, the erotic novel pursues an impossible goal: 'To escape our limits, to go beyond ourselves'" (49).[11] The implicit author's theories also establish that due to the close relationship between eroticism and topics such as desperation, violence and death, in a true erotic novel there must be a chapter full of pain. Thus, the gentleman, in his desperation, wanders among tombstones, hearses, and burials. In the same line, in a passage in which Madam X complains about her dissatisfaction both with masturbation and with her sexual gratification with others, she confesses her sadistic tendencies: "if you wanted to be the willing victim of a little sadism, the other came tenderly like a dove" (18).[12] She actually pities people who ignore the secret pleasures of sadomasochism and mentions a friend of hers who enjoys being whipped. In fact, she and her domestic assistant Marie are constantly pinching and verbally abusing each other throughout the text; Madam X even hits, kicks, and bruises Marie. The presence of violence in the text is not only real, but also imagined: in one passage a jealous Marie waves her scissors as she daydreams about castrating her nemesis Jonathan.

More importantly, the text plays several times–implicitly and explicitly–around the notion of rape. In the opening of the novel, for example, the omniscient narrative voice describes the gentleman's signature as an "alphabetical rape" (7)[13] that went violently up and down to end in spasmodic dots made by ink stains, simulating an ejaculation; later the narrator insists: "the spatial rape and the ink blotches, investing them with an allusive symbolism" (14).[14] Later, in a more explicit scene, a man violently rips Madam X's dress with a switchblade and then forces her to have sex with him against her will. Accordingly, the narrative voice explains: "the inevitable occurred, although Madam X didn't want it to" (25).[15] The confusion had arisen after the protagonist asked Marie to invite her suitor to the house. Unaware of the true identity of the gentleman, the injudicious maid decides to ask the friendliest of the men who were observing Jonathan publicly masturbate after contemplating Madam X's beauty. But the question remains, why would a woman writer choose to approach the concept of rape in such a frivolous way? Foster claims that this type of text constitutes a clever undermining of patriarchy:

> If it is true that feminism must deal with the way in which women not only accept their own subjugation by a phallocentric society, but also reproduce it in their own cultural production, either out of cynicism (the exploitation of the exploiter) or out of desperate self-defense (pretend to go along with the exploiter to forestall greater exploitation), then it becomes easier to explain why women might sign texts that can be claimed to be the very paradigm of the violent patriarchy. (Pornography 287)

Indeed, Gambaro is ironically rewriting previous erotic or pornographic texts in which scenes of rape or reminiscent of rape, or other kinds of sexual violence represent the paradigm of patriarchal fantasy. According to this critic, the feminist dimension of this novel is provided by "Madame X's assumption of the role of doer as the result of her frustrated awakened desire" (Pornography 293). Indeed, she challenges the traditional passive role of women in pornographic texts by becoming the active pursuer of pleasure, while the exhibitionist gentleman repeatedly fails to fulfill his promise to consummate the encounter, as he is thrilled precisely by this very postponement of the penetration.

In order to balance the violence that usually appears in erotic novels–the implicit author explains–writers recur to the use of poetic exploration, along with the typically pathetic humor that can be elicited from sexuality. Evidently, not much poetry can be found in this particular case; however, obvious humor emanates from hyperbole, obscenity, scatological sexual scenes, and filthy descriptions of underwear and bodily fluids. In certain scenes, for example, Jonathan's supernatural ejaculation soaks the faces of Madam X and her coachman or breaks windows in the hospital. In other sardonic passages aimed at ridiculing male sexual fantasies and exhibitionism, the gentleman has ninety-nine orgasms simply because he has smelt Madam X's curl, or, unable to control his deranged excitement, he scratches his entire body with the roses sent to the hospital by her. Throughout the text, his exploits and physical appearance are parodically described either within the semantic family of boats and sailing or in terms of the Spanish conquest of America: "the conqueror astride her dismounted after enjoying the fruits of America X without recompense" (11).[16] As Faser de Zambrano explains:

> Through parodic practices, *The Impenetrable Madam X* not only shows a failed copy of the male search romance, but it reveals the Columbine paradigm itself to be a copy as well, whose fictionalization and mythologization integrates perceptive and representative coordinates that are fundamentally imaginary. (154)[17]

In effect, his phallic exhibitionism symbolizes that of men in general, who have ineluctably disappointed Madam X since they "dismounted more precipitously than she esteemed opportune" (11).[18]

Madam X's immoderation is caricatured as well: she becomes so aroused when she is about to meet her suitor that it often smells like something is burning under her skirt. Page by page we learn that the domestic servants' image of Madam X is radically different from her own self-image. In fact, numerous scatological scenes underline the fact that her manners are at the very least questionable: she spits food, picks up wax from her ears, stumbles over her skirt while running downstairs, and, in accordance with the times in which she lives, she does not bathe very often, as she believes that water damages the skin. Moreover, in order to combat her boredom and impatience while her would-be lover recovers in the hospital, the protagonist pushes her loose tooth until it falls out. Suddenly, Marie puts it in her mouth, plays with it for a while, and then spits it out, hitting Madam X in the eye. More concerned with satire than with the verisimilitude of the story, the narrative voice explains that it took Madam X some time to extract the tooth from her irritated eye. Eventually, she will lose two more teeth and fracture her ankle. The lack of realism is increased through the use of anachronisms, such as mentioning the Statue of Liberty and the Eiffel Tower before they were built or political ideologies that did not yet exist. Like a few other characters in the plot, Madam X is the last descendent of an elegant and aristocratic family. Yet, once again, the narration purposely creates an atmosphere of inverisimilitude and triviality by inserting sentences in English in the original version in Spanish, such as "and so on," or by substituting boring and long descriptions of family trees with the word "etc."

Suddenly changing the grotesque tone into a vein of semi-serious social criticism, the narrative voice criticizes the fashion trends of the time, always dictated by men's desire, and clarifies how the protagonist ignores that in future times women would keep on feeling young until they are in their fifties or later. Soon, lesbian overtones begin to govern the protagonist's monologues, who confesses her desire to enjoy a body just like her own (that is, the body of a woman): "She regretted that her body was incapable of splitting into a woman-man or woman-woman; she'd have liked to feel her own weight and not another's, penetrate and feel herself penetrated, be both yin and yang" (18).[19] The transvestism that characterizes a costume party to which Madam X is invited intensifies sexual ambiguity in *The Impenetrable Madam X*. Once again alternating a humorous tone with a more philosophic reasoning, the narrative voice justifies the morality of lesbian sexuality and argues that repressed desire is the cause of many catastrophes in the world:

> There was an ocean of repressed desires, imprisoned and paralyzed, boiling in the depths of feared perversion. Or perhaps perversion was innocent and permissible: possession, love exercised as a service contract, cautious pleasure without risks, tradition that authorized love only between opposites was the real perversion. Born of hypocrisy it was suffocating from taboos. (84)[20]

Later, the narrator attacks the presence of guilt in every sexual exchange, including masturbation, which stops people from enjoying the world. Yet, this momentary seriousness is counterweighed by the lack of verisimilitude in the attorney's words during the trial of Jonathan, who is being accused of killing fifteen people as a consequence of his gargantuan ejaculation. In his determination to seduce the gentleman, the crazed attorney tenaciously attacks heterosexuality:

> How long will humanity allow heterosexual passion to provoke such disasters? How long will we permit such outbursts from two sexes that are

so different psychologically and biologically that they cannot harmonize with each other even if they try? (101)[21]

The attorney insists that men and women are incompatible and tries to prove that male homosexual sex is more fulfilling. For that purpose, he denigrates female sexual organs. Suddenly, he takes off his clothes, bites Jonathan on the mouth and tries to seduce him, while the courtroom undergoes an unstoppable orgy that involves most of the people present at the trial.

As was mentioned above, at times the narration becomes carnivalesque, but not only through attacks on male erotic fantasy. Approaching the end of the story, Madam X begins to feel older and decides to take off her indolent mask: while she still finds Marie very attractive, she no longer feels beautiful and the presence of the gentleman, whose name she does not even remember, no longer excites her. When, overwhelmed by insecurity, she asks Marie about her own physical appearance, the maid sees an ordinary and very deteriorated lady that has gained a lot of weight. Earlier, she had silently commiserated Madam X's foolish expressions and pathetic nursery rhymes when she thought about her gentleman. Yet, despite her unbearable character, Marie sees her inner beauty and tells her that she looks beautiful. She cannot explain the reasons why she still feels attracted to her mistress; however, she enjoys Madam X's docility, her generosity in bed, and she feels moved by her transparent wickedness and her naive presumption that she is that which she cannot be. One day, when Madam X returns home and realizes that Marie is not there, she cannot help but dearly miss her company. As usual, she acts in self-denial but feels jealous thinking that she might have slept with Jonathan.

Throughout the story we are repeatedly told about Marie's melancholic sadness and jealousy upon realizing that she cannot compete with Jonathan. She even dreams that she is naked in bed, weeping, while Madam X and her suitor ignore her existence or walk over her. Conversely, now she and Madam X mock the sexual incapacity of a passive Jonathan, who is lying down on the floor complacent with his own orgasm, and the women are the ones that jump over him in pursuit of their own sexual gratification, thus reversing Marie's dream. An exuberant Marie celebrates the illusion that she will no longer have to share Madam X with anyone and that perhaps she will find her feelings of love reciprocated, despite the fact that she is considered a vulgar lower-class person. Surprisingly, when the reader expects a romantic happy ending in which lesbian love triumphs over an evasive heterosexual intercourse, the possibility of a stable lesbian relationship is, as it happened in Marta Traba's *Mothers and Shadows*, once again postponed. Marie is saddened by disappointment when Madam X abandons her newfound sexual fulfillment for a new chimerical romance, immediately upon receiving a new letter from another mysterious gentleman. To the maid's surprise, an impatient Madam X pushes and scratches her, demanding that she pick up the new suitor's letter. Resigned and humiliated, she has to obey, lamenting the fact that she will have to cope once again with her lover's repressed sexuality. With this return to a new epistolary relationship, the novel takes on a circular structure that ultimately negates the possibility of an undisguised lesbian love affair.

Within the analysis of sexual identities, it is clear that while in Marie's case the affirmation of her individuality lies in her physical and sentimental relationship with her mistress, the latter's sense of belonging is achieved through class identification and through her obsession with being attractive to men, despite her obvious lesbian sexual tendencies. In any case, as Foster indicates, "the reliance on a structure of simple inversions in *Lo impenetrable* cannot provide for the opportunity for Marie as an alternate sexual sign to play any significant role other than as antiphonic to her mistress's ridiculous erotomania" (Pornography 296). This satiric rewriting of erotic novels written by and for men is the outcome of Gambaro's realization that she would never be able to write according to the traditionally male canons of the patriarchal and violent sexual fantasies that characterize the genre. It stands as a literary effort that partially fills the vacuum of this type of cultural production in Latin America. However, the apparent legitimacy of a lesbian discourse that defends homoeroticism at the same time that it denounces homophobic sexual politics is ultimately negated by the very burlesque tone used to caricature male sexual fantasies.

NOTES

1. "El uso de la perversión sexual como metáfora sería el resultado de la violencia que la sociedad misma alienta, en la medida en que el escritor se convierte en un canal de expresión del discurso mismo que él denuncia, un sujeto-objeto de lo aberrante que constituye su temática. En una sociedad patriarcal y autoritaria, la única manera del placer exacerbado es la perversión, y los autores canalizan por medio de la escritura esa agresión perversa" (232).

2. "El amor sexuado entre mujeres es más reprimido en estos sistemas donde a veces lo gay hace de florero en la fiesta eufórica neoliberal."

3. "Peor todavía imaginarla en luna de miel. ¡Vaya nombre imbécil para una simple violación!" (94-5).

4. "Quizá porque ahora, después de tanto dolor, sea posible acercarse a la literatura como a un lugar de esparcimiento, un lugar donde la imaginación, el desenfado y la desacralidad, sean pequeños aportes a una sociedad más lúdica y permisiva."

5. "Sabe y acepta que entre nosotras no puede haber el menor contacto, la menor relación, porque aparte de la diferencia social, hay un muro insalvable que es la identidad de sexo" (48).

6. "El encanto del caballero había sido su mástil prodigioso" (142).

7. "¡Gracias Dios mío! Ahora lo comprendo!" [. . .] "Lo impenetrable es la fuente de todos los placeres, porque no hay un placer sin incógnita" (147-8).

8. "Enlazadas por la cintura, saltaron sobre el cuerpo del caballero que estaba caído a un costado de la cama y como tantas veces, pero en esta ocasión con una consciente alegría que las exaltaba, las alumbraba mutuamente decidieron, graciosas y desenvueltas, adentrarse, gozar de lo posible. Penetrarlo" (150).

9. "Como en un cuadro, funcionan como 'trompe l'oeil' y no tienen, dentro de la estructura del relato, más imporancia que éste" (83).

10. "Como una figura marginada, que habla y actúa de una manera desafiante, logra reconfigurar el discurso colombino definido por la diferencia de género y sostenido por la heterosexualidad obligatoria, a través de una estratagema combativa: la lesbianización" (128).

11. "La novela erótica, como el erotismo, persigue un fin imposible: 'Salir de nuestros límites, ir más allá de nosotros mismos" (51).

12. "Si se deseaba ser víctima complaciente de un poco de sadismo, el otro venía tierno como una paloma" (20).

13. "Violación alfabética" (9).

14. "La violación de los espacios y los manchones de tinta, a los que cargó de un simbolismo alusivo" (14).

15. "Pasó lo inevitable, aunque Madam X no lo deseara" (27).

16. "El conquistador encima de ella, pero descabalgado después de usufructuar a América X sin dar ninguna recompensa a cambio" (13).

17. "A través de prácticas paródicas, *Lo impenetrable* no sólo muestra una copia fracasada del romance de la búsqueda masculina, sino que revela el paradigma colombino en sí ser (sic) también una copia, cuya ficcionalización y mitificación integra unas coordenadas de percepción y representación fundamentalmente imaginarias" (154).

18. "Descabalgaban más precipitadamente de lo que ella estimaba oportuno" (12-3).

19. "Lamentó que su cuerpo no se desdoblara en mujer-hombre, mujer-mujer, le hubiera gustado sentir su propio peso y no otro, penetrar y sentirse penetrada, ser el yin y el yang" (20).

20. "Había un océano de deseos reprimidos y no se les daba cauce ni se les concebía la obra, permanecían hirviendo en las profundidades de la perversión temida. O quizás la perversión fuera inocente y lo permitido: la posesión, el amor ejercido como contrato de servicios, el placer cauto y sin riesgos, las costumbres que sólo autorizaban el amor de los opuestos, fuera la perversión real. Nacía de la hipocresía, se ahogaba en lo contrariado" (88-9).

21. "¿Hasta cuándo la humanidad va a tolerar que la pasión heterosexual provoque estos desastres? ¿Hasta cuándo el desborde de dos sexos tan distintos, psicológica y biológicamente, que no pueden armonizar aunque lo pretendan?" (105).

WORKS CITED

Faser de Zambrano, Wa-Kí. "El discurso colonial/poscolonial y el erotismo en las novelas de dos escritoras: reedición del encuentro, conquista y colonización de América." May 1996. Graduate College of the University of Iowa.

Foster, David William. *Cultural Diversity in Latin American Literature*. Albuquerque: University of New Mexico Press, 1994.

_____ . "Pornography and the Feminine Erotic: Griselda Gambaro's *Lo impenetrable.*" *Monographic Review/Revista Monográfica* 7 (1991): 284-96.

Gambaro, Griselda. *Ganarse la muerte.* Buenos Aires: Ediciones de la Flor, 1976.

_____. *Lo impenetrable.* Buenos Aires: Torres Agüero, 1984.

_____. *The Impenetrable Madam X.* Trans. Evelyn Picon Garfield. Detroit: Wayne State University Press, 1991.

Pizarnik, Alejandra. *La condesa sangrienta.* Buenos Aires: López Crespo, 1971.

Reati, Fernando. *Nombrar lo innombrable.* Buenos Aires: Legasa, 1992.

Traba, Marta. *Conversación al Sur.* Mexico D.F.: Siglo XXI, 1999.

Illustration by Tonya López-Craig

The (In)visible Lesbian:
The Contradictory Representations
of Female Homoeroticism
in Contemporary Spain

Jill Robbins

SUMMARY. This article positions lesbian literature within post-Franco Spanish literature, demonstrating how works by Spanish lesbian authors and/or with lesbian themes have been marginalized publicly and academically, even after the liberalizations that have dramatically transformed Spanish society since the death of Franco. The article calls for a more thoughtful reading of lesbian literature in particular, and women's literature in general, providing a model with its encapsulated readings of works by Marosa Gómez Pereira, Ana María Moix, and Lucía Etxebarria. *[Article copies available for a fee from The Haworth Document Delivery Service: 1-800-HAWORTH. E-mail address:*

Jill Robbins is Associate Professor of Spanish literature, culture and film at the University of California, Irvine. Early studies focused primarily on gender and power in poetry, but more recent articles encompass the implications of trans-Atlantic connections in the dissemination of gendered national identities in Spanish and Latin American markets, through literary anthologies during the Franco dictatorship, and later through the strategies of the globalized publishing business. Her book, *Frames of Referents: The Postmodern Poetry of Guillermo Carnero*, was published in 1997 by Bucknell University Press, which will also publish her edition, *P/Herversions: Critical Studies of Ana Rossetti*.

[Haworth co-indexing entry note]: "The (In)visible Lesbian: The Contradictory Representations of Female Homoeroticism in Contemporary Spain." Robbins, Jill. Co-published simultaneously in *Journal of Lesbian Studies* (Harrington Park Press, an imprint of The Haworth Press, Inc.) Vol. 7, No. 3, 2003, pp. 107-131; and: *Latina Lesbian Writers and Artists* (ed: María Dolores Costa) Harrington Park Press, an imprint of The Haworth Press, Inc., 2003, pp. 107-131. Single or multiple copies of this article are available for a fee from The Haworth Document Delivery Service [1-800-HAWORTH, 9:00 a.m. - 5:00 p.m. (EST). E-mail address: docdelivery@haworthpress.com].

10.1300/J155v07n03_09

<docdelivery@haworthpress.com> Website: <http://www.HaworthPress.com>
© 2003 by The Haworth Press, Inc. All rights reserved.]

KEYWORDS. Post-Franco Spanish literature, Spanish lesbian literature, Marosa Gómez Pereira, Ana María Moix, Lucía Etxebarría, queer theory

This essay will focus on the issue of the (in)visibility of lesbianism in post-Franco, post-transition Spain, particularly in relation to Spanish narrative. In the first section, I will examine the different manifestations of the simultaneous presence and repression of lesbianism in three Spanish literary markets, those aimed at: (1) presumably unsophisticated gay and lesbian readers; (2) "sophisticated," intellectual readers, who comprise a small percentage of the overall market for the book industry; and (3) a generalized readership looking for titillation in best-sellers. The second part of the essay will focus on representative texts of each category, in order to examine the ways in which they relate to sexual identity markers for women in the Spanish public sphere.

LESBIANISM IN THREE MARKETS

Although lesbianism was nearly invisible during the Franco dictatorship (1939-1975), both female homoerotic texts and less stereotypical images of lesbians have emerged in Spain in recent years. I will argue, however, that the representations of the lesbian and lesbian sexual practices in contemporary Spanish culture do not correspond easily with female or homosexual equality, but rather intersect problematically with questions of the market, cultural institutions, democracy, religion, and the public sphere in Spain, still dominated by masculinist and heterosexist norms.

Gayatri Spivak suggests that "the text (of male discourse) gains its coherence by coupling woman with man in a loaded equation and cutting the excess of the clitoris out" (191). This elision of female pleasure from the discourse on sexuality was particularly predominant during the masculinist Franco dictatorship, in which the conservative, military Nationalists sought to reconstruct the state, with the help of the Catholic Church, on the model of the family. In this scheme, the prevailing definition of female sexuality derived from the most conservative factions of Catholicism, which sought to limit women's sexual activity to reproduction. During the years of the Second Republic (1931-1936), female erotics had been linked to the Left in general, and specifically to the anarchist movement, which had promoted feminism, female education and free love. After the Left was defeated in the Spanish Civil War (1936-1939), the victorious Nationalists sought to erase all vestiges of liberalism and to recreate the structure of the state on the Catholic model of family. They therefore insisted on the Marianist determination of women's destiny as mothers and placed an exorbitant value on the hierarchical institution of the nuclear family, in which the father alone ventured into the public sphere, leaving the mother to regulate the private space of the household. The accepted sexual norm for women in this order was passivity during coitus, as Rafael Torres explains in *La vida amorosa en tiempos de Franco*: "La esposa decente, la verdaderamente honesta, debía reprimir toda excitación y todo sentimiento de placer cuando el marido la poseía, casi siempre a oscuras y muchas veces con el camisón puesto" [The decent wife, the truly honest one, should repress all excitement and all sense of pleasure when her husband possessed her, almost always in the dark and with her nightgown on] (96).[1] This concept was maintained during the Franco dictatorship not only by the institution of confession (Torres 96) but also by direct State mechanisms, including government policies promoting pro-natalism, laws against prostitution and "unnatural" sexual acts, state-controlled pedagogy in the schools, and the Servicio Social, a requirement that women hoping to study and work complete a program of social service that spread conservative sexual ideology throughout Spain. Such state controls on women propagated the concept of the female body as the property of the male, the object through which he legitimizes his identity as the father, passing on his name and property to a child he knows is his. As Spivak explains, "The institution of phallocentric law is congruent with the need to prove paternity and authority, to secure property by transforming the child into an alienated object named and possessed by the father, and to secure property by transforming the woman into a mediating instrument of the production and passage of property" (184).

Given that the predominant image of female sexual practice in Franco's Spain was reduced to a passive and strictly reproductive marital coitus, lesbian sexuality was unimaginable. Lesbians were simply invisibilized as "solteronas" [old maids] or "chicas raras" [strange or queer girls] generally characterized as women who failed to marry either because they were too ugly to attract a man, or because their personalities did not fit the norm of the "marriageable" women; that is, they were too independent, or not "cheerful" or submissive enough, as Carmen Martín Gaite suggests in *Usos amorosos de la posguerra española* [Love Practices of the Spanish Post-Civil-War Era].[2] It should not surprise us, then, that psychological, anthropological and sociological studies of homosexuality under Franco largely omit women. It might surprise us, however, how many still do, as do cultural studies and anthologies of "homosexual writers." The leading anthropologist of the contemporary gay scene, Oscar Guasch, omits women almost completely from his studies. His heterosexual female protege, Olga Viñuales, the only anthropologist to date to study lesbianism in Spain, can only report about the sexual practices confided to her by those lesbians who agree to be her subjects. It is questionable, at best, that these women would share intimate information with this "outsider." Indeed Viñuales herself admits that she had difficulty gaining the confidence even of those lesbians politicized enough to belong to the Catalan lesbian collective, who were her only subjects (22). Her study, then, is reduced to interviews with a very limited group within an organization whose purpose is to support lesbians and promote to the general Catalan community a positive image of lesbianism. As we would expect, then, the lesbian sexuality described in her book does not transgress the "acceptable boundaries" of heteronormativity, despite the fact that texts like Pat Califia's *Sapphistry* have been translated into Spanish and published in Spain in 1997, three years before Viñuales's book appeared.

It is ironic that, given her limited knowledge of lesbian sexuality, Viñuales has become one of the "experts" on lesbianism most interviewed in the Spanish media. Her visibility may be attributed to her "expertise" as a professor who earned her PhD with her dissertation on lesbianism, and to her heterosexuality, which makes her a less threatening figure to the general Spanish audience than one of the leading activists in the lesbian movement, Mili Hernández, who founded the gay bookstore, Berkana, and the gay publishing house, Egalés. Hernández has been a militant in the movement for decades, and she has also appeared on Spanish television. In contrast to Viñuales, however, she is lesbian, she conforms physically more to the stereotypical image of the dyke, and her expertise has not been accredited through any recognized academic institution. She is thus simultaneously a more threatening and a less reliable spokesperson than Viñuales in the eyes of the average Spaniard.

Viñuales, not surprisingly, is quite traditional in her field study of the "lesbian subject." However, queer theory, which eschews clear gender/sexual identifications, is not foreign to Spain, nor is it outside the purview of writers or serious scholars. Indeed, there are several younger Peninsular scholars who find its insights most relevant to questions of Spanish identifications, including a group at the Universidad de Vigo (including Beatriz Suárez Briones, Xosé Manuel Buxán Bran, and María Jesús Salinero Cascante), Alberto Mira, and the philosopher Beatriz Preciado, author of the *Manifiesto contra-sexual: Prácticas subversivas de identidad sexual* [Counter-Sexual Manifesto: Subversive Practices of Sexual Identity].[3]

Even the more politically radical Hernández has not been influenced by queer theory, however, and to the extent that she embraces a gay/lesbian identity politics, she is also traditional, despite her militancy. The "Salir del armario" books, published by Egalés, in fact, are affirmative, often pedagogical texts that aim to normalize homosexuality for "unsophisticated," "uncultured" gay and lesbian readers. The writer Luis Antonio de Villena criticizes the series as "literature" in an interview with Leopoldo Alas in the latter's *Ojo de loca no se equivoca: Una irónica y lúcida reflexión sobre el ambiente*:

> El público gay muy culto está en el armario, y son los que compran toda esa literatura en cualquier librería normal, no en Berkana. No van a los bares de Chueca ni a la librería gay porque no quieren hacer militancia de ese tipo. Los que van a la fiesta de la espuma en Refugio y al Shangay Tea Dance los domingos no son cultos, no compran libros. Es un error hacer promoción por ese lado, porque te van a comprar tres, le dije [a Mili Hernández]. Y ella me explicó que por eso está publicando en Egalés todas esas novelas, que se entienden porque son facilonas, para ver si logran que ese público inculto se aficione aunque sea leyendo historias gays muy elementales, contadas de una manera muy corriente. Yo le dije que, puestos a docencia, la primera labor que tendrían que hacer sería enseñarles su propia historia, que no la saben. (112)

> [The cultured gay public is still in the closet, and they buy gay literature at any normal bookstore, not at Berkana. They don't go to bars in Chueca {the gay district} or to gay bookstores because they don't want to do that kind of militancy. The gays who go to the "foam parties" at Refugio or to the Shangay Tea Dance on Sundays are not cultured; they don't buy books. It's a mistake to promote to them, I told Mili Hernández, because you'll only sell three books. And she explained to me that it is for that reason that they're publishing all those novels at Egalés, because they're easy to understand and they want to see if they can get those uncultured people to read, even if it's reading very elemental gay stories, told in a conventional way. I told her that, if she wanted to educate them, the first thing she should do is teach them their own history, which they don't know.]

Here, Villena suggests a hierarchical cultural split between gay intellectuals and sexually-frenetic "locos," a division that certainly exemplary lives might place in doubt. Indeed, David Halperin states clearly in *Saint Foucault: Toward a Gay Hagiography* that "much of the impetus for Foucault's late work on *pratiques de soi* came from insights into the transformative potential of sex which he gained from his experiences in the bathhouses and S/M clubs of New York and San Francisco" (160).[4]

Alas also complains that contemporary gay culture in Spain has the effect of homogenizing gay identities by presenting a single norm–unrefined, unintellectual, incurious (112). Alas's book itself, however, creates its own homogeneous ideal of gays as cultured intellectuals who place little emphasis on the body (thus his elevation of smoking to a "cultural activity"). His study thus performs its own silencing of difference.

Particularly silent in his text are women. This omission reflects the secondary role of the lesbian within the gay community as a whole, and it is a shadow of the deprecation of the feminine in the general intellectual community of Spain. The interview regarding Egalés and Berkana, for example, is between Villena and Alas; Hernández is never interviewed directly. What is more, despite the recognition that Hernández is performing an important pedagogical function, both Alas and Villena denigrate the sector of the gay community she addresses as uncultured party boys (both the Tea Dance and the "foam party" are for gay men, not lesbians), thus implying that Hernández speaks to a crowd that is beneath them, and ignoring that several of these novels are directed not at men at all, but at lesbians. One could productively critique the heteronormativity in "Salir del armario," but Alas and Villena do not deign to analyze those texts at all. In a final note of condescension, Villena expresses his admiration for Hernández by admitting that she is "una chica lista" [a clever girl] (127), a form of praise that infantilizes this powerful woman.

Some of the contradictions apparent in the gay book business and these assessments of it by "cultured" gay male intellectuals reveal the uneasy convergence in democratic Spain between reality and the idealization of the liberal public sphere in the post-Franco era. Eric O. Clarke explains in *Virtuous Vice: Homoeroticism and the Public Sphere* that:

> the principles of translation from private to public retained by the bourgeois public sphere have historically contradicted its own universalist, democratic ideals. While claiming to establish a "context-transcending" sphere through which to adjudicate competing interests equitably, the conversion from private to public has involved quite particular, context-specific determinations of value. (4)

This is clear in the valuation of certain identity markers over others by many gay male Spanish intellectuals, who seek to separate sexual and intellectual practices, and, with them, different qualities of gay males. They, in fact, attempt to distinguish themselves from the rabble, and they do not seem to recognize the normalizing practices of the cultural public sphere into which they hope to integrate themselves–that of the Spanish intellectual elite, which continues to be sexist, sexually conservative, anti-popular, and vehemently opposed to the incursion of capitalist practices in the literary market.[6] As a consequence, their own hierarchy of Spanish homosexuals omits women altogether, except as objects of their pedagogy–i.e., the "lessons" they give Hernández or lesbians in general on pages 211-215–or as objects of scorn, as in the case of "fag hags." These hierarchies are shadows of the "interestedness" of the public sphere, as Clarke describes it: "the very ideals of the public sphere have historically been attached to a quite particular subject position: the white Euro-American, educated, presumptively heterosexual middle-class male who owns property" (8).

Clarke notes that the public sphere thus engenders two important contradictions. "The first is the contradiction between the ideal and the historical reality of the norms defining publicity" (8). Secondly:

> To achieve integration within forms of public discourse, excluded groups must appear to conform to the standards of the "normal citizen" by which they were excluded to begin with. This does not just entail the erasure of difference, although this does occur; publicity's conformist inertia can also render forms of difference into, for example, nonthreatening entertainment . . . (9)

We see two kinds of "normalization" in relation to the pedagogical texts published and marketed for gay and lesbian readers. First, the lesbian novels in the "Salir del armario" series in fact represent the lesbian women as "normal citizens," often with children and eventually "married" to other lesbians, thus reaffirming the norms of the heterosexist public sphere. Second, Alas's and Villena's comments about the series reveal a desire to normalize the gay male writer within the "high" literature circuit by representing cultured gay men as creatures more akin to their straight male counterparts than to the party boys, who unthinkingly adopt U.S. norms and cultivate the body. Women are omitted from their efforts, much as they are largely eliminated from the Spanish literary sphere in general; ironically, women can only be normalized in that circuit by presenting themselves as "not women," which means, "men," as I will explain below. Otherwise they are always viewed as inferior writers and readers, producing literature suited only for pedagogical purposes or for the lesser intellectual demands of the mass market. Finally, the literary product for the mass market is the best-seller, and there lesbianism often becomes the "nonthreatening entertainment" that Clarke mentioned above, best-selling novels featuring titillating female homoerotic behavior that corresponds neither to identity politics nor to questions of gender power relations or gender identity.

These contradictions have historically held true in Spain, not only for the queer subject, but also for women in general, who, with very limited exceptions, were excluded from the public sphere altogether until recent times, and particularly from the sphere of high culture. Maryellen Bieder explains that it is for that reason that even the 19th century novelist and intellectual Emilia Pardo Bazán sought to erase gender from her work:

> Since virility is the hallmark of men's writing, it necessarily comes to encode literary merit. . . . To read a woman poet as exclusively feminine is not a sign of admiration for her but of her exclusion from literary value. To find that her writing verges into the territory of the masculine becomes a sign of her approximation to value. (108)

Laura Freixas, among others, claims that this gender prejudice, which perpetuates the myth of female intellectual inferiority, continues to predominate in Spain, which has admitted only one woman into the Royal Academy of language and letters. She explains that, to the extent that women have gained visibility in the Spanish literary world of late, it has been as the writers, publishers, promoters and readers of an inferior cultural product, linked to the massification of the media. What is more, the predominantly male critics in the Spanish media attribute defects in literary texts to the female gender of the writer or the readers. It is for this reason that women prefer to be read not as women at all, but as "universal," that is, male, authors. Freixas notes that:

> Es desalentador ver el tesón, el esfuerzo constante, nunca suficiente, siempre renovado, siempre inútil, con que las escritoras han intentado y siguen intentando desembarazarse de la imagen desvalorizadora que las persigue. Cuando acceden a la literatura, resulta que ser *literata* es ridículo. Cuando escriben poesía, han de demostrar que aunque son mujeres y escriben poemas, no son *poetisas*. Cuando consideran que su literatura tiene algo específico, han de apresurarse a aclarar que es *de mujeres*, quizá, pero no, ¡Dios nos libre!, *femenino* . . . y así hasta el infinito. Naturalmente, es perder el tiempo. Los bizantinismos lingüísticos son puro galimatías cuando las distinciones que pretenden establecer resultan ser contradicciones en los términos: es absurdo decir que algo es *de mujeres* pero no *femenino*, o al revés. Porque el problema no está en el lenguaje: está en el sistema de valores, y mientras éste no cambie, el lenguaje seguirá reflejándolo. Si una palabra se libra de la connotación peyorativa–o cae en desuso–, la misoginia se desplazará sobre otra. (92)

[It's discouraging to see the tenacity, the constant effort, never sufficient, always renewed, always futile, with which women writers have attempted and continue to attempt to free themselves from the devaluing image that pursues them. When they accede to literature, it turns out that to be women literati is ridiculous. When they write poetry, they have to demonstrate that they are women and they write poetry, but they are not *poetesses*. When they consider that their literature has something that is gender specific, they must rush to clarify that it is *women's literature*, perhaps, but not, God help us, *feminine* . . . and so forth to infinity. Naturally, it's a waste of time. The linguistic labyrinths are pure gibberish when the distinctions they purport to establish turn out to be contradictions in terms: it's absurd to say that something is *women's literature* but not *feminine* or vice versa. Because the problem is not in the language: it's in the system of values, and, as long as that doesn't change, language will continue to reflect it. If one word frees itself from pejorative connotations–or falls into disuse–misogyny will come to rest on another.]

If an author is not only female but also lesbian, the critical attention tends to fall almost exclusively upon her sexuality, either as proof that only "masculine" women write well, or to suggest that women writers are innately "perverse." Salacious suggestions of lesbianism among the leading women writers in Spain (including Gloria Fuertes, Rosa Chacel, Clara Janés, María Victoria Atencia, Ana María Moix, Esther Tusquets, Ana Rossetti) have appeared in Spanish newspaper articles, and they also circulate informally in literary circles.[7] The writers in question have found themselves in the position of defending themselves from what they correctly perceive as attacks on their credibility as artists, given that the articles in question reduce their work to biographical speculations, foreground the authors' bodies as sexual objects subject to the judgment of male observers, and present those bodies as perverse. Serious studies of lesbian sexuality and discourse in Spain are thus quite rare.[8] This double prejudice, against women writers in general and lesbian writers in particular, has led most women–whether they are lesbian or not–to decline comment on their sexual orientation or to deny repeatedly their lesbianism, and to eschew any relationship whatsoever between their work and their sexual identities.

Feminist and/or queer critics have tended to respect this silence as a gesture of support to the women in question, except when those women are already "out" as lesbians. This "gentleman's agreement," however, has had the unfortunate effect of contributing to the invisibility of lesbian women in Spanish literary history; even in the history of gay writers in Spain. Thus, the recent *Galería de retratos: Personajes homosexuales de la cultura contemporánea*

[Portrait Gallery: Homosexual Personages in Contemporary Culture] by Julia Cela does not include a single Spanish woman. Esther Tusquets, who has published several novels concerning lesbian relationships, is briefly mentioned in the introduction to Spanish homosexual writers (164), but she could not be included as one of them because she has repeatedly denied that she is lesbian or bisexual.[10] Luis Antonio de Villena's *Amores iguales: Antología de la poesía gay y lésbica* [Equal Loves: Anthology of Gay and Lesbian Poetry] contains the work of only 3 Spanish women, out of a total of 126 poets, dating from ancient Greece to the present.[11] These three poets–Gloria Fuertes (1918-1998), María Merçé Marçal (1952-2000), and Andrea Luca (b. 1957)–are unequivocally "out." Several unknown young Spanish males are included, but even Ana María Moix is omitted, not to mention poets who have chosen to remain in the closet, or who do not explicitly mention lesbian love and/or homosexual acts in their work. This, despite recent studies of the expressions of love among women of the Hermandad Poética [Poetic Sisterhood] in the 19th century, or the rediscovery of two lesbian writers of the 1920s and 1930s–Ana María Martínez Sagi and Elisabeth Mulder–by Juan Manuel de Prada, which he details in *Las esquinas del aire: En busca de Ana María Martínez Sagi* [Corners of Air: In Search of Ana María Martínez Sagi].

In general, "high culture" lesbian texts in Spain do not represent any stable form of female or lesbian identity, a logical strategy in the sexist literary climate of Spain. They thus reflect many current trends in queer theory, but they do not attract those readers looking for identity politics, or for a lesbian erotics that either conforms to cultural norms or leaves them in the privileged position of the voyeur.

We might conclude from these observations that, for the general public and the book industry, lesbian eroticism is still the marketing of the female body according to the norms of the male-dominated heterosexist public sphere. And the female body is still the limit of the female writer who would be taken seriously in Spanish literary circles.

In the following sections of this article, I will examine three representative narrative texts. Rather than provide an exhaustive study of the representations of lesbianism in contemporary Spain, I will limit my focus almost exclusively to "lesbian" narratives in the three principal markets targeted by major publishing houses and by independent editors in the gay community. My goal is to complicate what we mean by "lesbianism" in the book market by examining some of the often contradictory implications of the increased visibility of gay and lesbian culture in the Spanish public sphere.

OUT OF THE CLOSET:
UN AMOR BAJO SOSPECHA, BY MAROSA GÓMEZ PEREIRA

Un amor bajo sospecha [A Love under Suspicion], published by Egalés in 2001, is part of the "Salir del armario" series published by Berkana. It is a "novela rosa" [sentimental romance novel] that recounts the life story of Lucía, who begins her first-person narration in the present, and recalls her past in a series of analepses as she prepares to meet her son's fiancee, Marta, for lunch. Lucía had married a merchant marine in Galicia during the waning years of the Franco dictatorship and had three children with him before falling in love with Matilde, a local waitress. When Lucía's husband, Sebastián, returns on one of his rare visits home (he traveled nine months of every year), he immediately notices that his wife and Matilde are in love, and he takes that opportunity to confess to her that he is himself gay. He explains that, although he initially hoped to fall in love with her and be "saved" from his nature, he never felt passion for her. Finally, he suggests that they remain married to avert suspicion, but draw up appropriate legal documents to protect all involved (especially the children, whom he naturally adores) in case some accident should befall him on the high seas, and then, except for brief cameo appearances, he conveniently disappears from the narration.

The descriptions of Lucía's relationships with Matilde, Sebastián, and the children conform to most sentimental clichés regarding romantic love and maternity. This allows the author to represent Lucía as a "normal woman," despite her lesbianism, which in turn is presented as an unchangeable natural condition. Thus, while attempting to "legitimize" lesbian relationships as "natural" as opposed to "perverse," the text unwittingly endorses the concept of biological determinism that has so often been used to justify gender roles in heterosexual unions. Not surprisingly, then, the text draws a distinction between male homosexuality (and male sexuality in general) and lesbianism: men are shown to be more aware of their sexual orientation and more responsible for their behavior in relation to it than are the women. The result is often contradictory (though never problematic to any of the characters), especially given that this is a narrative about a working mother who becomes the head of a household run by women. For example, Lucía admits that, before marrying Sebastián, she had fallen in love only with women and in fact never felt any passion for her husband (8-9), yet she feels used and betrayed when Sebastián admits to similar emotions: "Me había usado a mí, también lo había hecho con sus hijos; los cuatro habíamos sido su gran tapadera . . . " [He had used me, and he had also used the children; the four of us had been his great cover] (36). But, then, she will use this same "tapadera" [cover] when she sets off to live in Madrid with her children and "Aunt Matilde," with whom she maintains a seventeen-year relationship. By the same token, she suspects that Sebastián's family and her own guessed that he was gay but hid this knowledge from her, hoping that it was just a phase and that she would "cure" him with her love (35). She recriminates them for not recognizing his true identity–"¿No se les pasó nunca por la imaginación que aquello pudiese ser lo que era, su verdadera identidad, y estar viviendo a mi lado una farsa y, por lo tanto, ser incapaces de ser felices?" [Didn't they ever imagine that could be what it was, his true identity, and that living by my side was a farce, and, therefore, we could never be happy?] (35)–but she does not blame her family for not recognizing her own homosexual identity, nor does she blame herself for attempting to hide her relationship with Matilde from her husband (and later, from her children). Sebastián, of course, was not deceived because, as a gay man, he was immediately able to perceive the truth when he met Matilde. Why, then, could Lucía not perceive that Sebastián was gay? She even admits that he was the man "que más me atrajo y al que yo también atraje" [who attracted me the most, and who I also attracted] (8), implying that there was a kind of unconscious recognition when they were courting. These confused identities and mis-recognitions suggest that lesbians were still invisible in the 1970s when Lucía began her relationship with Matilde, but they also reveal a continued belief in stable, "natural" sexual identity, a "true identity."

The presumed sexual ignorance of middle-class girls and the general invisibility of lesbianism during the Franco years might explain some of the mis-recognitions in the novel. For example, "everyone" suspected that Sebastián was gay, but nobody recognized that Lucía was a lesbian, even though she had an affair with another girl when she was a teenager (9). What is more, the same lesbian identity that was imperceptible to "straight" people was clearly visible to a gay man. No one else can see that the women's relationship is sexual because it is assumed that women, being passive, can only engage in sexual activities with an "active," male partner. As Antonio García Martín and Andrés López Fernández put it in *La imagen social de la homosexualidad en España* [The Social Image of Homosexuality in Spain]: "se observa . . . que es en el polo de lo masculino donde aparece la sexualidad y el deseo. Por contra, el lugar de lo femenino será el lugar de la afectividad y del no deseo" [it may be observed that it is in the masculine pole that sexuality and desire appear. In contrast, the feminine place will be the site of affection and of nondesire] (50). Companionship between women is expected, but sexuality is not even contemplated.[12]

Indeed, although sexuality between the women is implied in the novel, it is never described. Rather, the author employs imagery of the sea and the Galician landscape to portray nearly all of the emotions and sensations that the characters experience. Lucía and Matilde's first sexual experience is described thus:

> En sus brazos me sentí como una barca varada sobre una cala solitaria, de fina arena y olas suaves que me mecían acompasadamente, lamiendo mi madera algo resquebrajada por el sol, penetrando en todas mis hendiduras, refrescándolas, salpicándolas con pequeñas gotas juguetonas y saltarinas, entrando por todos los poros, por todos los nudos, y dilatando toda aquella madera estructurada en barca. . . . (18-19)

> [In her arms I felt like a ship stranded in a solitary inlet, with fine sand and gentle waves that rocked me rhythmically, licking my wood that was somewhat cracked from the sun, penetrating all my fissures, refreshing them, wetting them with small salty drops, entering all my pores, all my knots, and dilating all that wood shaped as a boat.]

Given that these images form part of a system of maritime imagery that pervades the entire narrative, they imply that sexual activity is only one aspect of lesbianism. The extreme conventionality of these metaphoric evasions also serves to normalize lesbian sex for a heterosexual readership, or for women who are just coming out and do not want to be considered or consider themselves "raras" [queer]. The description, however, covers up the actual sexual practices of the women, as do similar passages in "straight" romance novels, and it thus maintains the sexist norm of keeping women in the dark regarding the workings of sexual activities that they might not yet have experienced. At the same time, the conventionality of the passage inscribes lesbian sexual activities within the bounds of heteronormativity, excluding any possible "deviant" activities (sadomasochism, bondage, use of sex toys, anal penetration, fisting, etc.). Again, Eric Clarke's assessment of this phenomenon is helpful:

> With regard to eroticism, only those private vices that conform to a heteronormative moral code are translated into legitimate public virtues. Thus elements of queer life that do not conform to this code are expunged with little, if any, regard for the imaginative diversity of queer life. . . . Because the ideals of bourgeois publicity use unduly universalized moral codes to govern the distribution of equity, conformity to a historically particular, class-inflected, and often racially homogenized heteronormativity determines what precisely will and will not become valorized representations of queer life. (9)

Indeed, the relationship that the women subsequently form is also entirely conventional. Matilde, who works as a waitress before meeting Lucía, takes the role of the mother to the children because Lucía has a serious career as a designer and cannot spend enough time with them. Lest we imagine that Lucía thereby becomes "masculine," she assures us that "no dejé de maquillarme, de curvar mis cejas, de sombrear mis ojos y de perfilar mis labios, cosas que sigo haciendo, y que sin duda haré hasta que no pueda sostener ni las tenacillas ni el perfilador de labios en mis manos" [I did not stop using makeup, plucking my eyebrows, putting on eyeshadow and painting my lips, things that I still do and will no doubt continue to do until I can no longer hold the tweezers or the lipstick in my hands] (25). Lucía is also a perfectly loving and responsible parent at all times. Even when she falls in love with her son's fiancee, she resists the temptation until her children reveal to her that Marta is not, in fact, in love with Sebas at all, but rather the whole engagement has been a ploy on the part of her children to arrange a meeting between their loving mother and the woman they think would be perfect for her.

The novel ends with all parties happy, well-adjusted and successful, the message clearly being that lesbianism is normal and should have no negative consequences within the family or in society. These institutions are, in fact, upheld in this "novela rosa," albeit in a format that accepts, accommodates, and even celebrates the productive, nurturing lesbian.

LESBIAN (IN)VISIBILITY IN HIGH CULTURE: LAS VIRTUDES PELIGROSAS, BY ANA MARÍA MOIX

Several "high culture" Spanish writers of the post-Franco period–Esther Tusquets, Ana María Moix, María Mercé Marçal, Ana Rossetti, Clara Janés– have foregrounded female homosexuality and/or sexual ambiguity as a disruption to the structures of social order. Many of these authors, including the Uruguayan Cristina Peri Rossi, are linked to the publishing business, and specifically to Lumen, which Esther Tusquets directed from the late 1960s until 2000, when it was bought by Bertelsmann, and she was forced into early retirement. Lumen was one of the most important publishers of the late Franco period, the transition, and the 1980s, when it brought out not only the work of Spanish women in general, and gays and lesbians in particular–writers such as Tusquets herself, Moix and her brother Terenci, Jaime Gil de Biedma, Rosa Chacel, and Leopoldo María Panero–but also translations of key foreign novelists and theorists, including Virginia Woolf, Gertrude Stein, Iris Murdoch, Julia Kristeva, and Monique Wittig.

"Las virtudes peligrosas" [Dangerous Virtues], the title story in a collection published by Ana María Moix in 1985, exemplifies the epistemological questioning implicit in the representation of female sexualities in these high culture texts. "Virtudes" is not a pedagogical tale (or exemplary life) in the sense of the "Salir del armario" series, nor does it provide an image, normal or otherwise, of lesbian identity. Rather, as it weaves the tale of a fascinating, mysterious relationship between women, it provides a theorization of the disconcerting effects that perceived female autonomy may have on the patriarchal constructions of Western society.

The apparent love story involving two beautiful society women is narrated entirely by Rudolph, the son of one of them, who tells the story to Alice, a young woman who the women have hired to read to them in their old age. The women have never confided their history to anybody, and the entire short story may in fact be seen as an analysis of failed hermeneutics, as the details of the relationship remain stubbornly invisible to Alice, Rudolph, Rudolph's father, and ultimately the reader. Alice never speaks in the story, Rudolph attributes dialogue to her on the basis of his observations of her snooping in his mother's house. Rudolph himself has done his share of snooping–reading, in particular, his father's diary–and peeping through keyholes in his desire to explain the mysterious mirror trick that his mother and the other woman continue to perform. His narration, like his father's diary entries, represents his desire for closure, but the silence of the women and the invisibility of their contact frustrate all attempts to categorize and thus discipline them.

The story involves two women, now old and living in separate houses, joined metonymically only by the young girl, Alice, who reads to them and brings gifts from one to the other. These women became fascinated with one another in their youth while the husband of one of them, an important general, was away on a military campaign in Africa. Before he left, his wife had requested that he grant her a whim–to attend the opera on her own, rather than sitting in the royal box reserved for the highest-ranking generals and attachés of the King and their wives. When the general returns after a five-year stint, he attends the opera and sits in the box with the other military men, from whence he uses his opera glasses to observe his wife observing the other woman through her opera glasses. The other woman, dressed identically, also spends the entire evening gazing at his wife through her own opera glasses. The general, believing he has witnessed a public sign of indiscretion, dispatches spies–his military underlings–to obtain proof of infidelity, but they come back empty-handed. From this point forward, the general becomes obsessed with visualizing and naming the communication between the two women, who invariably reflect one another perfectly, often appearing in public places simultaneously, dressed invariably in identical colors and performing identical movements. He never finds any evidence of infidelity, or of any kind of communication between the women, but, even as he criticizes his wife's "feminine" curiosity, capriciousness, and vanity, he continues spying on and punishing his wife, although she obeys his every whim, to the point of abandoning the opera and the city altogether. Even secluded in their country house, the general believes he sees the apparition of his wife's double and hysterically shoots at it. In effect, he evidences only that he himself is curious, capricious, hysterical and vain, and that his accusations of his wife have more to do with his own character than her own (he did, after all, live in an exclusively male barracks in Africa for 5 years). The general's repeated reproaches of his wife's irreproachable image thus mark a gendered incoherence in Western epistemological systems and the social structures based upon them, including the marriage ideal, and this incoherence leads inexorably to his own madness. In other words, the other woman, the mirror image of his perfect wife, disrupts the function of the woman in Western symbolic systems, as Irigaray has explained it, as a mirror of male desire; the general goes mad when he sees what he interprets as his wife's desire for a representation of herself. His wife's unnamed and unnameable desire deconstructs the logic of patriarchy.

At the end of the story, Rudolph apparently provides the missing evidence of infidelity that would reconstruct the father's system. He tells Alice that he has observed his mother, through the keyhole of her bedroom door, rub her body with the objects sent through Alice by the other woman, and he offers this as proof of past physical contact between the women. It is slight evidence, indeed. Beyond that, however, it is clear that Rudolph is an unreliable narrator. At the very least, he has lied to Alice, telling her that the old woman's son, Rudolph, is conducting scientific research in Africa, when he is, in fact, in his mother's house. There is also considerable evidence in the text that, like his father, he possesses the "feminine" vices of curiosity, vanity, and hysteria. Above all, he is mad, ridden with guilt for his father's death, since the final impetus toward his father's madness was a pair of portraits Rudolph painted of the two women and hung in the living room, where they gazed at and mirrored each other, much like their subjects. He is desperate, as he himself reveals, to shift this blame to his mother and the other woman, whom he metaphorically reconstructs as serpents that metamorphose into the rope the general uses to hang himself. The scene he witnessed through the keyhole and describes to Alice could as easily be an hysterical hallucination as a verifiable truth. Alice, and the reader, are clearly left with a reasonable doubt.

The reader, and particularly the male reader, is implicated in this systemic breakdown of epistemology because the only narrators in the story–Rudolph and the general (in his diary)–are male. The women are silent, the mute mirrors of masculine discourse, and their connection to one another is simultaneously visible in their mirroring of one another, and invisible at its core. They remain the subjects of our hermeneutic efforts, but the truth of their relationship necessarily eludes all the "readers" of their signs. In this text, then, lesbianism is a visible specter, or an invisible reality, that haunts heterosexist society, marking the limits of interpretation and knowledge.

LESBIAN TEASERS IN THE BEST-SELLER: BEATRIZ Y LOS CUERPOS CELESTES, BY LUCÍA ETXEBARRÍA

Lucía Etxebarría is not simply the author of best-selling novels; she is a media phenomenon, a superstar of the book business who has fashioned herself as a spokesperson of the counterculture. She is especially critical of the effects that the beauty business (cosmetics, cosmetic surgery, diet aids) has upon the female body and psyche, but she also points out the hypocrisy of bourgeois culture in regard to drugs and alcohol, and she is an ardent foe of homophobia. She maintains a Website, and she has her own page on <ClubCultura.com>, where she espouses her opinions on sex, drugs, fashion, feminist issues, and the cult of celebrity.

Etxebarría's own celebrity adds weight to these opinions, and that celebrity skyrocketed after the publication of *Beatriz y los cuerpos celestes* [Beatriz and the Heavenly Bodies], winner of the Nadal Prize in 1998.[13] This novel, in which the young female narrator declares her love for two different women within the first 2 chapters, also gave Etxebarría–who has made public her sexual preference for men–an entrance into the gay book market, to the extent that all of her works are now featured prominently in gay bookstores and on gay-related Websites, as well as in mainstream bookstores, including the book outlet of the department store El Corte Inglés. Indeed the response to the novel shows that, although the narrator and protagonist of the novel, Beatriz, might well believe that "el amor no tiene género" [love has no gender], as the book jacket informs us–in contrast to her love interest, s–Cat, "lesbiana convencida" [committed lesbian], and Mónica, "devorahombres compulsiva" [compulsive man-eater] –Spanish readers are not so gender-blind regarding sex. Thus, when *Beatriz* won the Nadal, the headline of the article in the Spanish daily, *El País*, read: "La joven Lucía Etxebarría recibe el Nadal con una novela que trata de la iniciación sexual" [Young Writer Lucía Etxebarría Receives the Nadal with a Novel About Sexual Initiation], followed immediately by the subtitle, "'Beatriz y los cuerpos celestes' incluye relaciones lésbicas con Madrid al fondo" ["'Beatriz and the Heavenly Bodies' Includes Lesbian Relations with Madrid as a Backdrop"] (Moret). The article goes on to assure the readers, in the words of one of the jurors for the prize, that "No es una novela lésbica, aunque hay elementos de lesbianismo. . . . El tema sería más bien cómo la familia y un ambiente social determinado pueden condicionar la vida amorosa y sexual de una persona. Es también un canto a la libertad de poder escoger el tipo de amor que desees" [It's not a lesbian novel, although there are lesbian elements. . . . The theme is more about how the family and a determined social setting can condition the love life and sex life of a person. It is also a hymn to the freedom to choose the kind of love you want.]. The title of the newspaper piece in *El Mundo*–"El Nadal premia el erotismo y la 'carga poética' de Lucía Etxebarría" [The Nadal is Awarded to the Eroticism and "Poetic Charge" of Lucía Etxebarría]–was actually *preceded* by the declaration that: "La ganadora asegura que su obra será 'polémica' porque su protagonista mantiene relaciones lésbicas y además es drogadicta" [The winner assures that her work will be polemical because her protagonist maintains lesbian relations and is also a drug addict] (Maurell).[11] In fact, the lesbian content of the novel proved to be provocative in a way that lesbianism in novels by Esther Tusquets, Ana María Moix, and Cristini Peri Rossi had not. It stimulated readers, and it stimulated book sales.

If Moix and the other "high culture" authors question the epistemological bases of gendered Spanish identities, and if the "Salir del armario" books simply ratify the traditional gender identities with a lesbian twist, Echevarría performs a hybrid: she creates the illusion of transgressing societal norms without questioning their epistemological bases, thus appealing to Spanish readers who want to appear postmodern, but are not ready to forfeit the values of their own upbringing. The Spanish public, indeed, wants to see its country, not in the bleak, isolated, moralistic terms of Francoism, but as an ultra-modern cosmopolitan liberal state, now that it is a member of the European Union and a leading investor in Latin American economies. In the 1990s, this globalized "hipness" implied an acceptance of women's rights and a tolerance of difference, including different sexual identities. Beyond even that tolerance, gay culture has recently come to represent the epitome of trendiness, as Suzanna Danuta Walters notes in *All the Rage: The Story of Gay Visibility in America*, even if visibility also implies an increased vulnerability to homophobic violence.[12] "Trendy" is certainly an adjective that could be applied to *Beatriz*, with its irreverence toward moral codes, its allusions to global media and businesses, its portrayal of bathroom drug use in the posh discos of Madrid, and its knowing descriptions of gay bars and their clientele. The rejection of the false values and bleakness of Francoism culminates in the final chapters of the novel, which detail the sordid life Beatriz led in Madrid, despite her family's wealth, before her father sent her off to Edinburgh. The descriptions of her drug-addicted friends, the family neglect, and the attempted rapes read like a naturalist novel, and they can be conveniently used by the reader to blame the protagonist's confusion regarding her identity on the hypocrisies and perversions wrought by the puritanical moral codes of Francoism.

For all its anger and faux-postmodern trendiness, however, the novel does not really disturb the premises underlying Franco-era sentimental novels directed at women, a genre to which the subtitle–"Una novela rosa"–alludes directly. The text often employs the very conventions of the "novela rosa" (female protagonist, love interest, melodrama, suspense, pat resolution) to undermine the lessons regarding morals and values–virginity, self-sacrifice, austerity, family submission to male authority–that the genre sought to teach young Spanish women. The use of suspense as a structuring element, especially between sections, also alludes to "women's literature" by creating the illusion that the novel was published serially, as such literature often was in women's magazines. What is more, the structuring of time in the novel–repeated prolepses and analepses that whet the reader's appetite without really providing crucial plot details–also recall the narrative manipulations of that genre. The cleverness and irony of the text, along with the references to popular and high culture, suggest that it is meant as a postmodern parody of the "novela rosa." When the narrator fills in all of the gaps at the end of the text and explicitly states her criticisms of the contemporary Spanish family, however, the postmodern pretensions are dropped altogether. In other words, although the structure of the novel might provide the reader with the illusory sense that s/he is performing the kind of epistemological exploration characteristic of postmodern texts, the text itself impedes such an exploration by withholding information and by later providing that information, and, with it, closure. Readers thus enjoy the trappings of postmodernism without its unsettling implications.

Most disturbing for a lesbian poetics is the voyeuristic positioning of the narrator, the character who believes that "love has no gender." This postmodern concept of sexuality is severely undercut by the narration itself, which distances the narrator from the characters she encounters. This is her description, for example, of the lesbians in the bar where she meets her female lover, Cat:

> La mayoría llevaba el pelo corto y vestía pantalones, aunque también había alguna que otra disfrazada de *femme*, con falda de tubo y melena de leona. Si una se fijaba, acababa por comprender que existía una sutil demarcación de territorios. Las radicales resistentes ocupaban el flanco izquierdo, uniformadas en sus supuestos disfraces de hombres, fumando cigarrillos con gesto de estibador y ceño de mal genio, las piernas cruzadas una sobre la otra, tobillos sobre rodilla, en un gesto pretendidamente masculino. En la pista bailaban jovencitas más despreocupadas, que podían haber estado en una discoteca hetero sin llamar en absoluto la

atención. Una rubia bastante llamativa se había permitido incluso ponerse un traje largo y coquetaba con una pelirroja que se la comía con los ojos, mientras correspondía a la conversación de su amiga con una sucesión de carcajadas nerviosas y forzadas. (25)

[The majority had short hair and wore pants, although there were a few disguised as femmes, with tube skirts and lion manes. If you paid attention, you began to notice that there was a subtle division of territories. The radicals occupied the left flank, uniformed in their imitation man costumes, smoking cigarettes with the gestures of a longshoreman and ill-humored scowls, legs crossed with the ankle of one on the knee of the other, in a fashion that aspired to be masculine. On the dance floor, the carefree young things that were dancing wouldn't have raised an eyebrow in a straight disco. A fairly gaudy blonde had even allowed herself to wear a long dress, and she was flirting with a redhead who was eating her up with her eyes while attending to her friend's conversation with a succession of nervous, forced guffaws.]

The narrator herself is not at all implicated in these performed identities of butch and femme, but rather occupies a voyeuristic position, and readers who see this world through her eyes thus garner an inside look into "alternative" lifestyles without implicating their own identities. Etxebarría thereby satisfies their curiosity regarding these lesbian subjects from outside their world (like Olga Viñuales); confirms to them that most lesbians are indeed "strange," and simultaneously "turns them on" with a moment of charged eroticism. At times, the narration of lesbianism is only a titillation aimed at male readers, as in the following description:

Un dato gracioso que leí en un libro de texto: En la antigua Roma las bailarinas de Lesbos eran las preferidas para animar los banquetes. . . . Pero la fama erótica de las muchachas de Lesbos no se debía a sus habilidades acrobáticas, sino a otra especialidad: el sexo oral, que según los griegos había sido inventado en la isla. Una habilidad que las lesbianas se enseñaban las unas a las otras. (38-39)

[An amusing fact I read in a textbook: In Ancient Rome the dancers from Lesbos were preferred to enliven the banquets. . . . But the erotic fame of the girls from Lesbos did not come from their acrobatic skill, but from another specialty: oral sex, which, according to the Greeks, had been invented on the isle. A skill that the lesbians taught one another.]

This voyeuristic technique obviously does not challenge readers to confront their own prejudices, transform themselves or feel any responsibility for the violence that often befalls real gay people when they become too visible.

Indeed, although there is considerable violence against women in the novel, none of it targets lesbian characters for their sexual preference. The lesbians, in fact, seem to enjoy a freedom from male aggression, even when they display their affections publicly: "Paseábamos cogidas de la mano y todos los peatones nos dirigían miradas de soslayo. En parte, porque les resultaba chocante la imagen de dos chicas paseando enlazadas. En parte, porque las dos éramos jóvenes y guapas y daba gusto mirarnos. Yo lo sabía y me sentía orgullosa . . ." [We walked along holding hands and all the pedestrians gave us sideways glances. In part, because they were shocked by the image of two girls walking hand-in-hand. In part, because we were young and good-looking and it was a pleasure to look at us. I knew it and felt proud.] (23). Again, male readers are allowed a voyeuristic glance, without the slightest insinuation that this scene could provoke any violent outbursts of fear or desire. It is exclusively in straight bars and contexts that men become sexually aggressive in this novel, which allows all women readers to empathize with the characters' victimization, without having to problematize the clear distinction between living as a heterosexual middle-class woman or "out" as a lesbian.

Despite these contradictions, Etxebarría is a popular figure in gay culture. She is accorded respect and admiration, in part, because she publicly condemns homophobia, taking on a role that many lesbian authors have been unwilling or unable to perform. Like Olga Viñuales, she does not threaten straight men and women in the general public, and she is not herself threatened by any negative publicity regarding her sexuality, which might adversely affect her marketability.

CONCLUSIONS

The increased visibility of lesbianism in Spanish texts, rather than pointing to some essentialized lesbian subject or even to real lesbian practices, reveals the contradictions of sexual identities both in the Spanish public sphere in general, and in the elitist literary sector of it. It is not clear if these contradictions can be resolved. Indeed, we might agree with Clarke's definition of the "subjunctive mood" of the public sphere:

To the extent that its ideals have been articulated as irreducibly counterfactual, and therefore on their own terms *must* remain contradicted by their historical manifestation, the public sphere can only ever asymptotically approach any consistency with these ideals, even as such consistency remains an operative, indeed demanded, pretension of publicity practices. It would therefore seem that the public sphere will always have a need to "self-correct." (9)

The texts I have analyzed here, and the public image of their authors, suggest a separation between idealized representations of sexual identities and certain realities, including (1) public opinion as represented by book sales and imagined in marketing ploys; (2) the valuation of male-authored texts over female-authored texts in Spanish "high culture"; (3) the deprecation of the body by the male cultural elite, tied to a tendency to separate abstract, masculine rationality from the feminine, irrational body; and (4) the continued linking of approved sexual practices to family values, particularly in the case of women.

The general public, gay or straight, prefers those texts that do not really question or problematize the structure of society or interpersonal relationships. This attitude could be seen as a legacy of the authoritarian Franco era, or as a holdover from the transition to democracy after Franco's death in 1975, when Spanish democracy was still fragile and needed to be defended at all costs from a possible resurgence of reactionary forces only recently displaced from power. The ideal of the liberal public sphere could not be tainted by imperfect realities in those circumstances, and those who suffered acutely fighting for the imagined rights and freedoms of liberalism under the authoritarian Franco regime were understandably reluctant to criticize its failings. Those who had the fewest freedoms under Franco–including homosexuals and women–rightly celebrate even their semi-invisibility today, their occasional ability *not* to be seen as the inferior sex or the perverse sexuality. Occasionally, however, this means that they must erase difference, be seen as "just like" men, or straight men, certainly never as women, lest their accomplishments be devalued or attributed to a degraded, U.S.-style, late-capitalist culture, even by many powerful gay writers. This partial visibility, represented in Moix's short story as a subversive virtue, a double negative that makes a positive, points to the sexism underlying the public sphere in general, and particularly in Spain. It is a condition even more grave than the elision of difference wrought by the normalization of homosexuality, which Clarke discusses, because lesbian writers are not even "normalized," but rather "neutered" and silenced, in Spanish "high culture." Even if their literature addresses the gendered foundations of "high" and "low," in their public lives they accept the credo that culture has no gender as the price of admission to the boys' club. The voice of the public lesbian in Spain–outside of the exclusively gay/lesbian market–thus falls to self-declared straight women, who perpetuate the very heterosexist structures that lesbian writers seek to undermine discursively: the nuclear family, the female body as sex object for the male voyeur, puritanical morality, the equation of women's literature with inferior popular culture. The workings of the Spanish public sphere make it difficult to imagine other options for lesbian authors, other than the "outing" of continued sexist and heterosexist practices in Spain, which the present article has sought to achieve.

NOTES

1. Torres goes on to note an ironic consequence of that norm: unsatisfied marital partners often sought extramarital sexual pleasure, with either lovers or prostitutes. He dedicates an entire chapter of his study to the various forms of prostitution during Francoism.

2. See in particular chapter 2, "En busca de cobijo."

3. Ricardo Llamas and Fefa Vila explain queer theory for Spanish readers in the article cited at the end of this essay.

4. See also James Miller's *The Passion of Michel Foucault* (New York: Sino and Schuster, 1993) and David Macey's *The Lives of Michel Foucault* (London: Hutchinson, 1993).

5. See my forthcoming article in *Iberoamericana*, cited at the end of this essay.

6. On one occasion, for example, gossip circulated about Ana Rossetti and a young female lover when, in reality, she was sharing a hotel room with her daughter Ruth. Personal interview with Ana Rossetti, July 6, 2002. Similarly, there have been unconfirmed rumors of a relationship between María Victoria Atencia and Clara Janés–which both women deny–and between Clara Janés and Rosa Chacel.

7. For an example, see María Jesús Salinero Cascante, "El cuerpo femenino y su representación en la ficción literaria," *Piel que habla: Viaje a través de los cuerpos femeninas*. Ed. M. Azpeitia. Barcelona: Icaria, 2001, 39-76.

8. Personal interview with Julia Cela, July 20, 1999.

9. Cristina Peri Rossi was born in Uruguay, but she has lived in Spain and France since her exile in 1972. She has collaborated with Esther Tusquets in the publishing business in Barcelona.

10. Terry Castle, in *The Apparitional Lesbian: Female Homosexuality and Modern Culture* (New York: Columbia UP, 1993), puts it thus: "When it comes to lesbians . . . many people have trouble seeing what's in front of them. The lesbian remains a kind of 'ghost effect' in the cinema world of modern life: elusive, vaporous, difficult to spot–even when she is there, in plain view, mortal and magnificent, at the center of the screen. Some may even deny that she exists at all" (2).

11. Her first novel, *Amor, curiosidad, prozac y dudas* (Barcelona: Plaza y Janés, 1997) was successful, but it sold many more copies after *Beatriz* became a hit, and it has now been made into a motion picture, despite some controversy regarding possible plagiarism ("Me han hecho mucho daño, pero tengo la conciencia muy limpia" [They Have Done Me a Lot of Harm, But I Have a Clear Conscience], interview with Leandro Pérez Miguel, *El Mundo*, October 2, 2001).

12. Beatriz, the protagonist, does experiment with drugs (cocaine and ecstasy), but it is her childhood friend, Mónica, who is the drug addict.

13. She also notes that with this visibility comes a high incidence of homophobic violence and condemnation of homosexuality by religious groups. The same dichotomy may be seen in Spain, where, despite greatly increased intolerance, many still believe that homosexuality is perverse.

WORKS CITED

Alas, Leopoldo. *Ojo de loca no se equivoca: Una irónica y lúcida reflexión sobre el ambiente.* Barcelona: Planeta, 2002.

Bieder, Maryellen. "Gender and Language: The Womanly Woman and Manly Writing." *Culture and Gender in Nineteenth-Century Spain.* Eds. Lou Charnon-Deutsch and Jo Labanyi. Oxford: Clarendon, 1995. 98-119.

Califia, Pat. *El don de Safo: El libro de la sexualidad lesbiana.* Trans. Carlos Benito González and María Elena Casado Aparicio. Madrid: Talasa, 1997.

Castle, Terry. *The Apparitional Lesbian: Female Homosexuality and Modern Culture.* New York: Columbia UP, 1993.

Cela, Julia. *Galería de retratos: personajes homosexuales de la cultura contemporánea.* Barcelona: Egalés, 1998.

Clarke, Eric O. *Virtuous Vice: Homoeroticism and the Public Sphere.* Durham: Duke UP, 2000.

de Prada, Juan Manuel. *Las esquinas del aire: En busca de Ana María Martínez Sagi.* Barcelona: Planeta, 2000.

Etxebarría, Lucía. *Beatriz y los cuerpos celestes.* Barcelona: Destino, 1998.

Freixas, Laura. *Literatura y mujeres: Escritoras, público y crítica en la España actual.* Barcelona: Destino, 2000.

García Martín, Antonio and Andrés López Fernández. *Imagen social de la homosexualidad en España.* Madrid: Asociación Pro Derechos Humanos, 1985.

Gómez Pereira, Marosa. *Un amor bajo sospecha.* Madrid, Barcelona: Egalés, 2001.

Halperin, David. *Saint Foucault: Toward a Gay Hagiography.* Oxford: Oxford UP, 1995.

Macey, David. *The Lives of Michel Foucault.* London: Hutchinson, 1993.

Llamas, Ricardo, and Fefa Vila. "Spain: Passion for Life. Una historia del movimiento de lesbianas y gays en el estado español." *conCiencia de un singular deseo: estudios lesbianos y gays en el estado español.* Ed. Xosé M. Buxán. Barcelona: Laertes, 1997. 189-224.

Martín Gaite, Carmen. *Usos amorosos de la posguerra española.* Barcelona: Anagrama, 1987.

Maurell, Pilar. "El Nadal premia el erotismo y la 'carga poética' de Lucía Etxebarria." *El Mundo.* Internet Edition. January 7, 1998.

Miller, James. *The Passion of Michel Foucault.* New York: Simon and Schuster, 1993.

Moix, Ana María. "Las virtudes peligrosas." *Las virtudes peligrosas.* Madrid: Alfaguara, 1998. 11-51.

Moret, Xavier. "La joven Lucía Etxebarria recibe el Nadal con una novela que trata de la iniciación sexual." *El País.* Internet Edition. January 7, 1998.

Robbins, Jill. "Globalization, Publishing, and the Marketing of 'Hispanic' Identities." *Iberoamericana.* Forthcoming.

Salinero Cascante, María Jesús. "El cuerpo femenino y su representación en la ficción literaria," *Piel que habla: Viaje a través de los cuerpos femeninas.* Ed. M. Azpeitia. Barcelona: Icaria, 2001. 39-76.

Spivak, Gayatri. "Displacement and the Discourse of Woman." *Displacement: Derrida and After*. Ed. Mark Krupnick. Bloomington: Indiana UP, 1983. 169-95.

Torres, Rafael. *La vida amorosa en tiempos de Franco*. Madrid: Temas de Hoy, 1996.

Villena, Luis Antonio de, ed. y prólogo. *Amores iguales: Antología de la poesía gay y lésbica*. Madrid: La Esfera de los Libros, 2002.

Viñuales, Olga. *Identidades lésbicas*. Barcelona: Edicions Bellaterra, 2000.

illustration by Tonya López-Craig

Index